SPICY BITES

CHAINS

2018

ROMANCE
WRITERS
of Australia

Chains 2018: Spicy Bites Anthology

Anthology of Short Stories published by Romance Writers of Australia Inc © 2018

Print ISBN: 978-0-9872809-7-8

Ebook ISBN: 978-0-9872809-8-5

Spicy Bites Coordinator: Jayne Johnson

Cover design by Lana Pecherczyk

Edited by Sarah Gates

Proofread by Claire Boston

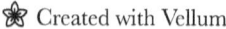 Created with Vellum

Other Spicy Bites Anthologies

Tattoo: Spicy Bites Anthology 2017

SPICY BITES

CHAINS
Short Story Anthology
2018

Contents

Foreword

The word chain can have such negative connotations and many common sayings reflect that: Don't yank my chain, a chain is only as strong as its weakest link, or a ball and chain symbolising imprisonment. But it can be so much more than that too.

A chain can be a connection—to an event, to a commander, to a loved one. Necklace or bracelet chains can be given as gifts, or are links to our history when they are passed down the generations, and the types of chains are almost endless: paper chains, daisy chains, bicycle chains and snow chains just to name a few. There are so many opportunities to bring chains into a story.

Our authors in this year's anthology have switched the negative into a positive, with chains being very much integral to their erotic stories. From BDSM to necklaces, snow chains to bicycle chains, tattoos, weapons and leads, they have incorporated chains seamlessly into their stories.

I am sure you will enjoy what they have come up with.

Happy reading!

Claire Boston—President RWA 2017-2018

Unchain My Heart

BY MELANIE PAGE

TEN FEET away stood a goddess in welding goggles.

Her head was a thick fleece of inky curls, glinting in the sunbeams from high windows. A sheen of sweat gleamed on taut, tan arms. The silver tee was rubbed and scorched; but for that, Tom would have assumed it was painted on. It clung to every generous, double D curve. Her black jeans were hotter than pitch.

He watched as she tilted the oxy torch. The brilliant blue tongue of flame licked over the heavy links of chain. Showers of sparks rained down. Then it shut off and she pushed at her forehead with the back of one slim wrist. He felt hot just looking at her.

'I'm looking for R Rawley?'

The oxy-wand clanged against the gas cylinder as she jumped and turned. She pushed the goggles up into her hair and faced him.

'I'm Rae Rawley.' Her words were matter-of-fact, but the voice was a sultry summer cocktail. 'Can I help you?'

He kept his voice studiously neutral. First rule of business; don't leap on the customer. 'Tom Catchpole, from All

That Glitters. You sent an email about buying surplus chain, old stock…'

'Of course!' She came over, hand outstretched. A shard of memory pierced his brain.

'Raine Rawley, by any chance?' Damned if she'd looked this sexy in senior.

The polite businesswoman smile splintered and a real one took its place. 'Of course, Tom Catchpole. You were at Sunny Coast High.' Their hands met and her eyes swept over him. 'Looking good, Tom.'

'Likewise.' There was a pause, as if each were assessing the changes of the last decade. He turned, took a mental step back. Nodded. 'I've gotta say. This is incredible work.'

His eyes took in the double height shed, its rough timbers and trusses topped with corrugated iron. While each end had a mezzanine area reached by a flight of stairs, the central vault was given up to a glorious melange of metal, a piece of industrial style art that nonetheless had beauty to burn.

A female form was suspended from the ceiling, larger than life by a generous measure. Her arching spine was a series of links, large enough to have anchored the Titanic. Tresses of rusted iron chain flowed down her back. Her torso, arms and legs were cleverly fashioned from a mix of heavy aluminium and bicycle chain, among other things. She hung from black ropes and, at the lowest point, a Perspex plinth kept her stable and anchored.

'That's spectacular.'

She glowed.

'I take it she's why you're in the market for chain.'

A swift upward glance and a shrug. 'I use it a fair bit, but not usually precious metal. That's something of a first.'

He gestured upward. 'Tell me what you need.'

WHERE TO BEGIN. Rae Rawley, artist and business-woman, was fighting a losing battle with lust. For the first time since she'd begun 'Unchained Heart,' her mind wasn't on the job. Her high school crush had waltzed into her workshop and her control was slipping. Hah! She gave herself a mental shake. Slipping my arse. Shot all to hell and going down in flames. She needed a cold drink. A cold shower would be better, at least until she had a little privacy, but a drink would have to suffice.

'Can I offer you a drink? We can talk in my office. It's cooler.'

His eyes flickered over her, in a way that she might have misconstrued as interest if she wasn't a) filthy and, b) so not his type. She knew his type. Long legged surfer chicks who put out. He'd been a nice enough guy in school, but he'd looked right through her.

She held out one hand in invitation.

'That'd be great.'

Rae's office was no more orderly than usual; photos of designs past, sketches of designs future and the chaos of a present spent welding, rather than a tidy space. Tom said nothing except 'thanks' when she handed him a Coke and gestured to the ancient vinyl sofa.

'Will you be selling her… it?'

She took a swallow of water, welding dried her out. 'She's commissioned. Two weeks from now she will hang in the entrance gallery of the Hinterland Art Gallery.'

'Well, congratulations! I'd imagine that's quite an honour.'

She flushed, pleased that he understood something of her delight. But kind words didn't pay bills, Dad always said.

'It is, but it's good business for them too. A local unknown who is prepared to give them the art, for less than it's worth, to be displayed.'

'And for you an opportunity to get recognition.'

A tiny smile. 'Pretty much.'

'So, your email?'

She nodded. 'She's almost finished. The main elements are in place, as is all the structural work. What I'm looking for is fine, bright silver chain to delineate her face, shoulders, bust. And gold for the heart.'

'Two weeks?' He looked out through the one-way mirror into the main space. 'Had you always intended to approach us?'

She shook her head and reached up, running frustrated fingers through her hair. She might have imagined it, but he blinked and took another swig of his drink. 'Originally I'd intended to go around the second hand shops, pawnbrokers, that sort of thing. But I kept putting it off, busy with the work. And time got away. Chain of similar grade and quality will look better anyway.'

He stood. Rae felt her heart sink a little. But hey, he hadn't been interested back then and nothing had changed. Besides, he probably had a wife and two-point-four rugrats. He put out a hand and held hers for three long seconds. She counted.

'I'll see what I can do for you, Rae.'

HE'D BEEN nine kinds of idiot, Tom told himself, fishing in his pocket for the car key. His hand brushed against his enthusiastic cock and he bit back a groan. Hiding under a shapeless Sunny Coast tunic and shy smile had been the hottest body in the district. He'd been blind.

Five minutes ago, he'd almost made a fool of himself. As she'd run her hands through her hair, every muscle in her perfectly toned body screamed his name. He turned on the engine. What he wanted was to sit in the car and ease his frustrations, but it might be a little hard to explain to passersby. Hopefully, an hour in the back room sorting old stock would dampen his ardour. And give him a good excuse to come back.

HE RETURNED about a half hour before sunset. She felt his eyes on her back where she knelt under the statue, doing fine welds on the knees and calves. The light was behind him, its dying rays cut through the fine cotton business shirt to the broad chest beneath. He'd taken off his jacket and rolled up his sleeves. He took the packing crate he was carrying and set it next to the door of her office.

'I'll be ninety seconds.'

'No worries.'

When she stashed the equipment, he was leaning nonchalantly against the wall. The crate at his feet held packets and spools of chain in various grades.

'I'm glad you're still here. I was hoping to catch you before you went home for the evening.'

She laughed. 'Home is about eight feet, straight up. You couldn't miss me. Come in.'

She switched on the desk lamp and he took his place on the tatty sofa. In the soft light, the years fell away. Finally she was alone with the guy she'd had the most humongous crush on. And he wasn't just a teenaged hottie from maths anymore; he was lean... sharp... sophisticated. Whatever 'it' was, he'd got a bulk discount.

'You always live on-site?'

'My parents are pestering me to move home... It's not safe, blah blah blah. You know how it is. But I got fed up with paying more than I could afford for a boring flat I never used.'

He seemed a little on edge, in the shadow between dusk and lamplight. And she remembered the rugrats.

'But you probably need to get home to your family. How did you want to do this?'

He shook his head. 'I've got nowhere I need to be. I was actually going to ask you if you wanted to catch up over dinner.' Her reaction must have given him pause. 'It doesn't have to be tonight. Unless... Sorry. I shouldn't have assumed.'

'No, I'm free.' Uncool, Rae. Don't sound so desperate.

'Is that fancy free or free tonight?'

Her smile snuck out when she wasn't looking. 'Ah, can I choose box number three?'

'Both?'

He grinned. Ah, there was the old Tom Catchpole, with the megawatt charm that had every girl in Year Eleven desperately in lust with him. Unexpectedly, there was a pang of hunger that had nothing to do with food.

'You'll want to have a shower. What time should I come back for you?'

She considered. 'If you are happy to wait, there is wine in the fridge and a TV upstairs.'

'If I won't be in the way, that would be great. Would you like me to call Le Relais in Flaxton and see if they have a table?'

She felt oddly flattered. 'That would be amazing.'

Rae led him up the stairs beside her office. Fortunately she didn't use her minuscule lounge room often enough to mess it up. She poured two glasses of Riesling, handed him the remote, grabbed a towelling robe from the bedroom and slipped out.

THE TV WAS ON, but no political chicanery or salary cap scandals could distract him from the sound of running water. He pressed mute and closed his eyes. Having a shower involved Rae taking her clothes off, stepping into the water spray. She was going to soap up, lather creamy bubbles onto that café latte skin of hers—throat, arms, breasts… He leaned back in the recliner and surrendered to the images playing in the darkened cinema of his mind. He didn't touch himself. Oh, he wanted to, but he wouldn't be inclined to stop. So spending a couple of hours in a restaurant with a telegraph pole in his pants might be awkward. The bubbles would rinse off, running down the vee of her body, over the buttocks that looked as ripe and firm as a peach…

The sound of running water was coming from behind him. But that was where the screen door led out to a small verandah, looking over the back of the shed.

He rose, drawn by the oddity of the situation. Seconds took him to the door and beyond it, to look out over the cleared land as it fell away to the creek, fifty metres away. The last of the tangerine light from the sinking sun peeped from between nearby gum trees. The sound of his steps was drowned out by the water and the shrieking of cockatoos.

Raine had an outdoor shower. A set of metal stairs had been welded onto the side to the shed. A headhigh semi-circle of corrugated iron, with a hedge of murrayas planted around the outside, protected her privacy from any roos that might be hopping past.

But not from him. Where he was, high on the outside wall, he was unseen, free to watch at his leisure.

Looking down, he could see her back and shoulders turned towards him, those perfect breasts hidden. She had her fingers working her hair into a lather, working him into a lather, her skin gleaming. And then she turned, her head tipped back to rinse, her body exposed to his gaze. She opened her eyes.

THERE WAS a figure up on the dark verandah, and Rae didn't need three guesses to work out who it was. The glimmers of light from the television reflected off his white shirt, daubing him with moving splashes of colour in the almost dark.

She had two choices. She could perform the dance of the outraged virgin; cover up the bits that mattered and shout at him to go away. Or…

She closed her eyes again and rinsed, lifting her hands into her hair to get the last of the suds out, giving him a spectacular view, if she did say so herself. Then she turned away and squeezed a generous amount of body wash onto the loofah that she used. Very deliberately she worked it over her upper body. She turned her back on him and bent over, washing below. Then she twisted and turned in the spray, running her hands over the wet skin, sluicing the foam away. This was a one-night-only performance, and he might as well get his money's worth. Besides, she was enjoying herself, in a naughty, thrill-seeking kind of way. She turned back towards the verandah, eyes closed, head tilted. Her last action was to slide her hands up her body, over her belly, ribs. She lifted her breasts high, ran her fingers over the nipples. Then she turned off the water and, wrapping herself in her towel, brought down the curtain.

BY THE TIME SHE DRIED, dressed and climbed the stairs, he'd put the soiled hanky back in his pocket, zipped his fly and got his breathing under control.

'Did you manage to get a table?' She kept her voice matter-of-fact, running her fingers through her hair, scrunching and air-drying the onyx curls. The air smelled like sex. Her lips twitched.

'For seven thirty. Will that give you enough time?'

'Plenty.' She disappeared through the swing door and into her bedroom. She gave a sultry smile at the girl in the mirror before applying a flick of mascara and a nude lip gloss. She dabbed rose oil on her pulse points and pushed some bling into her ears. Her favourite dress was black, patterned with silver cobwebs, it would go well with… She picked up the silver mesh rose on a fine chain and walked back out to the lounge.

'Would you mind giving me a hand with the catch?' She put the rose to the hollow at her throat and draped the chain over both shoulders, then turned her back to him. His fingertips barely touched her skin, but she felt his breath on the back of her neck, the heat of his body inches away.

'It's my pleasure.'

She felt his hands move away. The chain settled around her throat. She leaned back and smiled into his eyes.

'That's good to know.'

'YOU KNEW that I was on the verandah, didn't you?'

The waiter had just cleared the empty crème brulèe dishes. Their table by the window looked down on the valley lights and, for a moment, it seemed that she was distracted by the view, that she wouldn't answer. Then her lips curved slightly and he knew.

'What can I say? I like to leave a good impression.'

'Believe me, I'm impressed.' He considered for a minute: her poise, the seductive undertones, the cat-with-canary-feathers smile. And then he matched these with his memories. The girl in them was brash and laughing, without an ounce of guile. Whether on the netball courts or in class or sauntering between classes, her arms full of books but her mind far from them, the opinions of others mattered less to that Raine than the gum under her shoe. This siren smile was a mask.

He left the events of the evening hanging. 'So, apart from a fine arts degree and your welding apprenticeship, what have you been up to?'

'Nothing much.' She turned warm eyes on him. 'What about you. What did you do before you bought the business? I would have imagined you settling down.'

'Not for lack of wanting.'

'Really?' Now he had piqued her interest. He didn't normally open up on a first date, and some things were better left alone, but she wasn't exactly a stranger.

'After I got out of the army, I got a job driving trucks interstate. The money was good, it gave me a chance to save. And I met a girl. Well, a woman.'

'Okay.' The watchful expression told him that she was skipping ahead to the end of his story.

'We became an item. And as she already had a flat, I just got into the habit of hanging out there, on the one day of the week I was home. It suited me. I had a home base. It suited her. She had a busy lifestyle and so she did her thing six days out of seven and on the seventh we relaxed. And then, when we'd been together about three years, I micro napped at the wheel one day and somehow parked my semi in the middle of a canola field.'

She gaped. This was the real Raine, not the seductress of the past hour. 'What happened?'

'I was so shaken up that I drove to my destination and phoned my boss to tell him that I quit. And I flew home.'

'And she wasn't pleased, even though you were safe?'

'She asked me where I was going to stay.'

'Oh Tom!'

He signalled for the bill. 'She did me a favour. She taught me to look past the shiny wrapping, to the worth of the gift.' He reached out and placed his fingers over her hand that was laying, palm down, on the table. It was strong, capable, covered in tiny nicks and scars from the welding torch. It was real. It was perfect. 'I'll take you home.'

She looked up at him. The sex kitten was gone, her dairy-milk eyes were shining. 'Thank you, Tom. It's been a lovely evening.'

'I'd like to drop by, see how your sculpture's getting on. If that's okay.'

'It's more than okay.'

EIGHT DAYS later

Gold chain looped up and back, slowly knitting itself into a hollow gleaming heart, the size of Raine's clenched fists. She sat hunched, as she had for the past two days, laying the links in position, applying the pure gold solder, repeat. The silver was in place, the face that of a lovely girl, etched in delicate silver links.

She'd made one change. Instead of the sultry downcast gaze she had planned, she'd given her creation eyes that looked out at the world with hope—open to opportunity, confident and bright. In her hands was the last piece of the puzzle: the gold heart that would stand out from the breast, bursting out, breaking free of the chains that reached fruit-lessly after it, unable to recapture it or lock it down again.

Link… solder… link… solder… link… solder… done.

With her own heart firmly in her mouth, she carried the dainty object into the centre of the shed and, with trembling fingers, secured it to the fine rod, anchored firmly in the centre of the chest. It needed to appear as though it were floating free. She pulled her hands gingerly back and stepped away to get a more complete view. Then, as she'd promised, she pulled her phone out of her pocket and let her thumbs dance across the glass.

It's finished.

Is it incredible?

It's freaking awesome!

Give me ten minutes.

He was there in eight. He pulled up right outside the doors and stepped into the shed where he'd first seen her working, looked up at her, staring in delight.

'Congratulations, Raine. You've made magic here.'

She threw herself into his arms, one arm around his waist, the other around his neck. 'I've really done it. Oh, my God! I've finished.'

'She's magnificent. Once she's polymer coated and installed at the gallery, you'll be able to celebrate.'

Raine just looked at him. 'I can't wait that long.' She took a step back, her hands criss-crossed at her waist. With a single movement the t-shirt came off. The expression on his face was encouragement enough. She shucked off her jeans, put her hands to the knot of his tie.

'Do you want to go upstairs?'

'Nope.' Her hands were busy with the buttons on his business shirt. Fortunately she was skilled with small, fiddly items. The shirt followed the tie to the floor. 'You have the most gorgeous chest.'

'Well, thank you.'

'My pleasure.' Her hands had found his belt buckle, found his fly. His pants hit the ground. She dropped to her knees.

'You don't have to… Oh, God.'

She stopped for a second. 'I do have to. Right now, or I'm going to burst.'

She took him again enthusiastically, his head sliding along the roof of her mouth, feeling the heat, every one of the tiny ridges. Her tongue slid up his length, caressing, while her hands played over his belly and thighs. His fingers laced themselves into her hair; he groaned.

The sound was sweet music to Raine. Her right hand came down and cupped him, gave the slightest squeeze. His response was everything she had ever dreamed. Until he stepped back, out of her hands. Out of her mouth. She felt herself pulled to her feet and then her mouth was full of his tongue, where his cock had been just seconds earlier. His hands played over her back and bum, fingers sliding under the elastic to grope her arse.

'You're greedy, Raine!'

'You love it.' Her voice was a low purr; the sex kitten had come out to play.

'I do. And so will you.'

He turned her then, so that the cleft of her bum was pressed against the missile jutting proudly out of his jocks. His hands splayed across her, one travelling slowly over her mons, the other cupped her breast, rubbing hard fingers over the nipple. His lips and teeth worried her neck, laid a minefield of kisses under her jaw.

She ached for it, ached for him. 'Please…'

She felt one finger insinuate itself under the elastic at her crotch and slide across her skin. She went weak at the knees.

'Now, Tom, please.'

'You are in a hurry, gorgeous. I've been waiting a week for this, since I saw you in that shower.'

'I've been waiting a decade for you.'

He switched sides, curling his chin against her throat, bringing his mouth to her lips. But he didn't kiss her. He paused. She opened her eyes.

'If you've been waiting ten years for me, Raine. I'd better make damned sure it was worth it.' She felt one hand spread over her belly, fingers wide and kneading, like a cat making a soft bed. The other took her throat and jaw and held it firmly. And then… Oh God, he was kissing her with a slow deliberate sensuality that threatened to put her back on the floor. Someone whimpered.

Eventually he slowed. Stopped. Disengaged himself from her mouth. Withdrew the tips of his fingers from her panties. He pulled his trousers up and lifted her, one arm under her knees, the other behind her back.

'I can walk.' Secretly she was ecstatic.

'I'm getting in practice. Because when I'm finished with you, you won't be able to.' They passed into her office and through the kitchenette. Tom slid open the glass door that divided the utility area from the back deck and shower. 'Remember when I was watching you?'

There was a small wary nod.

'Did you imagine what it might be like if I was in the shower with you?'

She could feel her face brighten as he slipped off shoes and socks, dropped his trousers, slid out of his briefs. One hand reached out to stroke him.

'Ah, Raine. You've had a turn. It's my go now.' He fixed his mouth to hers with more of the drugging kisses, but they were simply an appetiser. Unclipping her bra, the clever hands glided forwards and her breasts fell into them. His hot mouth branded each nipple as he suckled them in turn. Her panties magically disappeared.

'Shower?'

'Turn it on.'

He released her and her hands found the cool metal taps. He continued to stroke the length of her body while the water warmed. She stepped into the spray and he joined her, their wet bodies pressing together. His lips came down on hers again, his hands gripping her hard.

'I want you to wash yourself. Like you did before.'

Oh God. It had been an impulse before, but now—with his body calling to her—she trembled as she squeezed strawberry gel into the sponge. She kept her eyes closed, and slowly, seductively, soaped one arm, the other, drew the bubble-laded net across her breasts.

'I wanted to come down here and join you. I stood up there, watching you, the way you moved, the water running down your body.' His voice was as sensual as his kisses. It made love to her, penetrated her deeply so that she moaned. 'I was so hard. Like I am now. Then I had to go inside, come in my hand. But tonight, I'm going to come in you. In your hot… wet… sexy… pussy.'

She keened, her eyes still closed. She felt the sponge fall to the floor. One finger slid between her thighs. She buckled.

'Open for me, sweetheart.'

She half expected his hand. But it wasn't. The tip of

his tongue delved leisurely into her curls, traced her clit. She took a deep breath. And then he was suckling, drawing the morsel of flesh between his lips, rubbing it with his tongue. The heat of his mouth was a sensual furnace and he stoked it fiercely.

'Oh, God! I can't… No more.'

'Do you want me?'

Only more than life. 'Yes!'

HE TURNED OFF THE TAPS, wrapped her in a towel and led her back into the office. She looked around, as though bemused. 'You don't want to go to bed?'

Bed could wait. First there was another fantasy that he wanted to bring to life.

'When we came in here, you sat at your desk. All I could think about was you, and me, here on this old sofa.' He sat down, knees spread, his nakedness rampant, and drew her towards him. In his hand was a small foil packet. 'Put it on me.'

With trembling fingers she smoothed it over his cock. He turned her back to him and drew her down, onto him, one hand on each of her thighs, so that she was positioned astride his lap. Slowly, incrementally, their bodies made first contact.

'Come, honey, sit on my lap.'

He was halfway into her body when he moved his hands. One went to her clit, exposed for his pleasure, the other rolled one nipple, then the other. Her hips bucked and he pulled her down, tighter against him. He heard her breath catch as she impaled herself fully.

Tom waltzed his fingers over her sex and felt her writhe in delicious torment. He turned his lips to her ear.

'Do you love it, Raine? Do you love the way I fuck you?'

The tamped excitement broke over her like a wave. Her body clamped around him. She screamed and he felt the moment take him.

'IS THAT ENOUGH CELEBRATION FOR YOU?'

She hid her face against his bare chest, stunned into incoherence by the best sex in forever. A glimmer of memory stirred—at what she'd done, at what she'd said. I've been waiting for you for a decade. So cool, Raine. Why not say desperate and dateless? 'I never intended…'

He kissed the corner of her mouth, oh, so softly. 'I know you didn't plan that. But I did. I've wanted you since I saw you again, even before the shower. Why do you think I had a condom in my pocket?'

That was unquestionably true. Raine offered him a small shrug, her eyes bright, lips curving in a smile. 'I guess it will have to be sufficient celebration. I don't want to wear you out.'

'Oh, I have to prove myself, do I? Very well. Never let it be said that I wouldn't rise to the challenge.' He kissed the other corner of her mouth. 'But it might have to wait. I'm all out of condoms, and we have to go pick up our clothes.'

Out by the completed statue, hanging serenely from her ropes, Tom fastened his buttons, put his arm around Raine and drew her to him in a congratulatory hug.

'That really is magnificent work. I'm proud to have been even peripherally involved.'

She leaned into his shoulder. It was amazing, looking at the finished piece, how liberated she felt. It wasn't just atomic sex. It wasn't having someone else validate her work. It was the courage of her own convictions; the knowledge that her ideas had merit, the confidence that she had the ability to make it happen. And it was the willingness to go after what she wanted. Nagging uncertainty, the last of the chains that bound her, snapped. She turned.

'I could go for a little more celebration, if you're up for it.'

He gave a slow, sweet smile. 'You're on.'

'Your place…' She ran a hand over his bum. 'Or mine?'

'Well actually, there's this really great Thai place, in Nambour…'

Her eyes went wide. He chuckled. He actually chuckled. 'What, you were just planning on using me for sex, keeping me chained to your bed? Not that I would mind. But I thought we might take it slow, you know. Get to know one another.' He bent and kissed her, but not with passion —a salute of lips. His fingertips ran a slow caress under her jaw and chin. 'Who knows where it might end up?'

Unconsciously she ran her thumb where his lip had been. Yes, he was worth waiting for.

Daisy, Chained

BY JOSIE BAKER

KALIKA ALLOWS herself a small smirk at the flash of fear in her opponent's eyes. Royce has six inches and forty kilos on her, but she's got him where he's most vulnerable. His eyes flick down to his groin, to where the tip of a bamboo stick presses into the flesh protecting his femoral artery.

As the smallest built member of the 'club'—a haven her brother set up for his mates out the back of his converted warehouse apartment—Kalika is no lightweight fighter. Not one of the boys takes sparring with her and her sticks lightly.

Attendance is typically erratic, but most of her brother's mates have made the effort to be here tonight, and the comforting smell of male sweat swells with the rising temperature. They, and Kalika, are drawn by the promise of a treat—a visiting guest with a skill foreign to the club.

Hiro has driven out from Sydney where he has a waitlist of students eager to learn his technique. The air buzzes with anticipation and while they wait, the members fill the time sparring. Any pairing of the eclectic styles adopted by club members makes for an exhilarating challenge; a test of skill, flexibility, and nerve.

Royce is circling, looking for a weakness in Kalika's defence. He fights with empty hands, his size intimidating, but his lack of agility balances the contest. Kalika gives herself over to the dance, enjoying the absolute control of every muscle in her body, revelling in the power of her limbs and torso. Her senses are so attuned to combat that her reactions anticipate almost every move. The sticks have become extensions of her arms, lengthening the reach of her attack, strengthening her defence. She sways and whirls with lethal force.

Almost as gratifying as hitting her mark is the challenge of deflecting blows, limbs and, often, solid male bodies, with as little damage to herself as possible.

A parry morphs into attack, an intended strike to the neck blocked and reversed so Royce is forced to the mat, with her sticks pressed against his throat.

Distracted from her triumph by a prickling beneath her skin, Kalika turns slowly. She's used to being watched— admired by those who recognise her skill, scorned by those threatened by her unfeminine strength. But this attention feels different.

Kalika leaves Royce gasping for breath at her feet and locates the source of her discomfort. A slight man, tall but not heavy, standing upright but relaxed in the doorway leading from Jake's office. He is dressed in a white robe and looks more like a healer or philosopher than a warrior.

The combat around her seems to pause and night sounds of distant traffic and crickets drift in on the breeze through the open roller door. It only stops for a moment before grunts and thwacks of flesh on flesh resumes.

The dark-haired man in the loose robe nods and steps

into the room with Kalika's eldest brother, Jake, at his side. She plants her feet wide and stands straight as they head in her direction.

'Hiro, this is my sister, Daisy.'

'Kalika,' she growls and nods a curt greeting to the visitor. She tolerates the wimpy flower name at work, because she knows the customers at the beauty salon prefer a feminine, unintimidating receptionist. She needs the weekly payslip. 'As you can see, there are no flowers here.' Kalika scribes a half circle with her right arm to indicate their surroundings of concrete, exposed brick, industrial lighting, combat mats and sweat—lots of it.

'A pleasure to meet you, Kalika. Is your name in honour of your discipline: Kali?' Hiro nods at the sticks she habitually carries beneath her left arm.

'No. For the Hindu goddess.'

'Yeah. With those sticks of yours, you look like you've got more than two arms,' Jake says, with a laugh at his oft-repeated joke.

'It does seem appropriate. She's often illustrated with either four or ten arms. And standing on her partner, Shakti,' Hiro says with a smile, as if to soften Jake's teasing. Kalika's eyes narrow. She doesn't need anyone to defend her, especially a man who, although at least five inches taller and with a strong posture, appears physically weak.

'She's a warrior. A destroyer of evil. A goddess of violence and death. A symbol of female empowerment.' There was a lot to admire about the fearsome divinity who kept her consort subservient.

'She is also a benevolent mother, divine protector and bestower of liberation. Your skin is not blue, and I see no garland of human heads, so you must be the Kali Purana.'

Kalika's eyebrows lift. It isn't often she meets a guy who

knows his theology. Kali Purana is depicted as beautiful, her hair loose, body firm and youthful, riding a lion, four-armed and holding a sword and blue lotuses. Heat at the compliment blooms over her body and Kalika clenches her fists until her nails dig deep into her palms.

Don't let this guy's knowledge and flattery get under your skin.

Jake, bored with the conversation, turns to address the gathering of about twenty, most of whom are still sparring.

'Warriors,' he calls out. 'As you know we have a true master in our midst tonight. Are you ready to be impressed?'

Kalika huffs, doubtful that will be the outcome.

Gradually the grunts and blows of fighting subside and the crowd gathers around the central mat. When he has the attention of the crowd, Hiro calmly slips off his robe, folds it neatly and lays it on a black gym bag at the back of the mat. Kalika blinks, not quite believing what she's seeing. Beneath the robe he's dressed in a pale grey outfit that looks like silk pyjamas. What is her brother thinking?

From inside the gym bag he takes out a grey silk pouch and pulls out two short sticks as he strides to the centre of the room, tucking the empty pouch into his waistband.

Hiro plants his feet, takes a stick in each hand and a deep breath, and rotates his wrists. The sticks unravel and hit the floor, lengths of steel bars joined by short lengths of chain, ending with flags of silk—one black, one white.

Shoulders rolling, body sinuous as a snake, Hiro sets the chains to flight, the silk of his costume fluttering as if caught in a strong wind. The hard lengths of steel flowing from his hands become a blur and disappear, the only indicator of their location is the silk flapping at the tips.

The boys are silent, rapt by the demonstration of skill

and agility. Kalika, too, is mesmerised by the movement of his body—the chains as much a part of the man as his limbs.

Her mind wanders as she sways slightly, imagining herself inside his body and how his muscles must feel. Would they be light and free with the movement, or heavy with the effort of keeping the chains aloft? What does a man who moves so gracefully do with his time, when he's not whirling his whips? Does he go out dancing? Does he watch TV or read? Does he prefer men or women? Why is she even curious?

A series of acrobatic tumbles finish the demonstration and the boys whistle and clap their appreciation. Kalika claps along. She won't deny being impressed by Hiro's skill, but the man is not a warrior.

She steps forward as he folds the chains onto themselves with small flicks of the wrist.

'That was very pretty, but can they be used in combat?'

To the side of the mat, Jake shakes his head, embarrassed, but Hiro smiles and places the retired whips back in their silk bag.

He locks eyes with Kalika, unbuttons the silk shirt and slides it off. Her gaze drops to the pure muscle of his arms and torso. Now the shirt is gone, she can see there is nothing but flesh to cover the bulge of biceps, pecs and abs. Not an ounce of fat. Hiro folds the shirt and places it on top of his gym bag, the ripple and movement of muscles fascinating to Kalika. She's used to barely dressed men, but Hiro's body is a work of art, and even more naked without any of the ink decoration she is so used to seeing. From a side pocket he pulls out a folded chain whip with a scarlet flag.

Kalika moves into the breeze coming through the open

roller door—to cool down, not to get a closer view of his body, of his every move.

'A volunteer,' Jake calls out, enjoying the buzz of tension in the room. No one wants to mess with those chains. One of the whips alone could inflict serious pain and injury.

Erik, always wanting to be the toughest and strongest, steps forward with his curved kung fu broadsword and reluctantly puts on a face guard. Hiro nods his satisfaction with his opponent's choice of weapon—a traditional pairing for the chain whip.

'Against a whip chain,' Hiro begins, using the more traditional name for his weapon. 'You have the options of disruption…' He rolls his shoulders, then his torso, and the chain gathers momentum. With a tilt of his head and an encouraging expression, Hiro indicates that Erik is to block the swing of the chain with his sword as he moves to attack. Erik hesitates, afraid of the strand of steel whirling so close.

Hiro steps forward and strikes Erik lightly but often, trying to provoke him to attack. Kalika breathes heavily out through her nose in disgust at Erik's cowardice.

'Interruption…' Hiro indicates again for Erik to move into his swing. Infuriated by each humiliation, by each touch of the whip, Erik charges in. He catches the chain on his sword, clumsily. With minimal effort, Hiro wraps his chain around the sword, then Erik's arm, and with a twist of his shoulder, drops the wall of fat and muscle to the mat.

'Or entangling.' Hiro finishes with almost concealed impatience, his breathing barely accelerated. 'Anyone else?'

Kalika steps forward. The room goes dead quiet, as if everyone is holding their breath.

Erik drags himself to his feet and hands her the face

guard. She puts it on and takes her sticks from beneath her arm, swinging them to loosen her shoulders.

Hiro nods, a look of satisfaction in his eyes.

Kalika tenses the muscles of her rib cage, back and abdomen until her core is as hard as the steel she is about to face. Learning from Erik's lessons, she studies Hiro's movements and absorbs her opponent's rhythm into her body and her mind. Waiting for the right moment, she lunges forward and successfully disrupts the chain with her sticks. She moves against the momentum of the whip and tangles it, tries to pull it from Hiro's grasp, but the chain turns to liquid and slides from her grasp.

Breathing hard beneath the face guard, Kalika studies Hiro's face to judge his intention. His full lips are thin with determination and his beautiful almond shaped eyes narrowed. He cannot see her face, but he can see her eyes and he watches them intently. She may have failed to win the first encounter, but she knows she has ruffled her opponent's cool demeanour.

He begins another round of attacks, which she successfully blocks, until the chain is moving so fast it disappears. She watches his face, but Hiro's expression is blank, and she cannot judge his intention. A dart of pain on her thigh jolts her, not from the shock of the hit, but the flare of pleasure. Surely, she is mistaken. Being bested, and struck, can't possibly feel like that.

Hiro's nostrils flare with his victory. Kalika pulls off the facemask and throws it behind her. She needs to have full vision and judgement if she's going to disarm him.

The next hit catches her on the soft flesh below her ribs, unprotected by fabric. She gasps as pleasure surges through her body. The first hit was no anomaly. What is going on?

Kalika tries to disguise it, but she momentarily lets her

guard down, lets him best her with a snap to the bicep, wanting another taste of the pleasure/pain. Hiro raises an eyebrow slightly. He's glimpsed her response, and her intention. He knows she deliberately left herself open.

Kalika steels herself, determined not to weaken again.

The chain whirls around Hiro's body as he swings and sways. She nods at the knowing challenge in his eyes. She will not let the boys see her bested again, no matter how good it feels.

Determination has turned Hiro's face into a mask. He scales up his attack, as if possessed by some demon, determined to get another hit. The chain is invisible, the scarlet flag a blur in her vision, but she senses a strike coming, raises her sticks to block it. The end of the chain wraps around her upper arm. She absorbs the pleasure of the strike and embraces the pain. This is her chance. She drops one of her sticks and grasps the chain onto her arm, twists and rolls her body, her unexpected move jerking the whip from his hands.

Hiro bows to her in defeat and bends to pick up the whip handle. Conflicting feelings churn in her stomach. She should be elated with a victory over one so skilled, but confusion at her reaction to the stinging blows, and to Hiro, taints her triumph.

WITH THE DEMONSTRATION OVER, the boys make their way to the change room for showers.

Kalika looks around for Jake. They usually cool down together with a yoga session while the boys use the facilities. Unable to spot him, she shrugs, happy to be alone. It's her favourite time of the day—quiet, her body loose with fatigue. She hits play on the iPod in the corner and smiles.

Fleetwood Mac, just loud enough to drown out the horse-play in the showers.

She sings along to The Chain, words she knows by heart, as she stretches the soreness out of her muscles. The twinges where the whip has left welts on her skin remind her of pleasures inflicted. What would sex with Hiro be like? She almost wants to find out—to experience the clash of combat with him in sexual form. A contest of strength and strategy, with orgasm as the prize.

She will never find out. He is probably already on the road back to Sydney.

From the positions of downward dog, triangle pose, happy baby, Kalika nods to the boys as they leave, shouting goodbyes as they go home to wives, partners, families.

Home. She unfolds her body and stands, sighing deeply. She would end the night with the usual stir fry noodles and a rerun of Dexter.

When the last guy leaves the change room and closes the roller door, Kalika pads in for a shower. Jake will use the bathroom in his apartment upstairs, so this large room is all hers now, silent and dim, lit by a single bulb above a lone mirror. Hot, damp air engulfs her. It feels like a swimming pool change room—mirrors fogged to white and wet patches on the bamboo floor—but infused with cologne, not chlorine.

Kalika peels off her sweat-damp three-quarter leggings and sports crop, and unravels her bun, brushing her dark hair out, the tips caressing the bare skin below her shoulder blades.

Warm water flows over her scalp and face and cascades through her hair. Eyes closed, she pictures the way his body moved, swirling like the wind, like the water over her body, and how slick the chain felt on her skin. Soapy smooth hands run over her skin, her breasts, her stomach, between her legs. She groans.

Not here. Wait. Prove you are stronger than this need.

Kalika snaps off the tap and steps out to grab her towel, scrubbing her skin dry. Pulling the loose pants from her bag, her gaze catches on a flash of metal out of the corner of her eye.

A neatly folded chain whip pokes out of a black gym bag. It's his. He's still here. He must be in Jake's office.

She steps into the soft harem pants and glances at the doorway.

If a moment of contact can produce such amplified pleasure, how would it feel to have the chain wrapped around her skin? With the whip in her hands, she could control the sensation, extend the pleasure, bind herself tighter and take the pleasure higher.

Warmth floods her sex and she reaches for the handle, pulling out the folded weapon and unravelling the cold steel.

The end of the chain touches the floor and she lifts her arm, circling it around her body, round and round. She thinks of him, swaying, flowing, the steel an extension of his hard body, his muscles bunching and relaxing with each movement. She remembers the look in his eyes as he'd wrapped her in his chain, the tip flicking her skin with flashes of pleasure. Despite the lack of reaction on his face, his eyes had revealed his desire. He'd enjoyed watching her resist arousal.

The whip tightens with each circuit. Cold metal touches the skin of her belly, slides over her ribs like a snake and along the crease beneath her breasts. The touch of the chain on her nipple sends a shock of pleasure through her body, a path from her nipples to her sex. Her knees weaken and Kalika pulls hard, gasping as the links dig into her other nipple. She drags the chain over her skin, squeezing her erect nipples. Her breathing accelerates, and she wraps the rest of the chain around her breasts, catches the end of it and pulls tight, groaning with the bite of the now warm metal.

The muscles of her pelvis tense, her sex throbbing with need. She imagines how the chain will feel between her legs, hard steel over soft fabric, pressed against her clit.

Desperate to satisfy the yearning for release, to bring herself to orgasm with his weapon between her legs, she releases the end of the whip, so she can re-position the chain. Then she stops still, scalp prickling. She holds her breath and slowly lifts her gaze.

He is there, a slim silhouette in the doorway. By the height and physique, she knows it is him, not her built-like-a-bull brother.

'This time is allocated for female members to shower,' she croaks out, trying to speak as if she doesn't have his whip wrapped around her breasts.

'Please accept my apology. I didn't know. I came for my bag.' Hiro steps into the light, his torso still bare, silk pants hanging low on slim hips. She doesn't know how much he's seen but it's enough to interest his cock, which is unashamedly straining against the thin fabric.

His gaze, intense with interest, travels from her flushed face and taut neck, down her arms to where her fingers hold the whip, following the chain to her breasts, his gaze a caress. Her nipples tingle with the intensity of his focus.

He reaches behind and pulls something from the waist band of his pants. With a twist of his wrist the links unfurl, the scarlet flag at the tip waving like a bird's wing—the whip he used for the demonstration. He holds out his other hand and runs the links over his palm, slowly, deliberately —teasing her?

Kalika grabs the end of the chain that dangles against her belly and yanks it tight, gasping at the jolt of pleasure that surges through her.

Slowly, as he slinks toward her, Hiro swings the whip around his head, swoops it down so it circles his body, hissing through his teeth as the tip flicks his belly, his nipple. When she's in range, he flicks his wrist and the chain snakes out toward her, the end wrapping around her waist, a steel-tongued caress, before sliding away.

She steps towards him, wanting more, wanting the sting of force he'd shown her earlier.

One side of his mouth lifts and he steps closer, muscles bunching and the metal bites the swell of her buttock.

Her moan invites him to increase the force of his next strike. She pulls the chain tighter around her breasts, panting as Hiro's stinging caress quickens around her hips. His gaze is drawn to the bulge of her biceps, to her breasts, and he frowns. She glances down to see her flesh, swollen on either side of the chain, her nipples clamped and tormented. The pleasure that accompanied the torment has faded and she pulls the ends of the chain harder, chasing more, but it's not enough. She lets go. She needs to release the roaring desire that's trying to burst through her skin. She needs contact with her clit.

As he unfurls his chain from her lower abdomen, she grabs the end and uses it to jerk his body close, close enough to lift it over his head, to drop it behind his hips. She takes hold of the other side and jerks him hard against her. She groans with pleasure and pulls harder, grinding her sex against his erection.

Hiro's hands snake out and grasp her hips, steel beneath silk, stopping her movement.

'Be still.' The command in his voice dissolves any thought of protest.

Carefully, he unwraps the chain from her torso. Her body quivers, skin throbbing with the rush of returned blood to her breasts, her body lighter than air. She watches, rapt, as he lifts a padded mat from a hook on the wall and lays it on the central wooden bench. She shivers. What pleasurable torture is he preparing for her?

He comes back to her, guides her body so her back is against the wall and kneels, his face at her ribs, his breath hot on her skin. The command in his eyes when he looks up keeps her still and silent, while he slides his hands beneath the waist band of her pants, pushes the fabric slowly down her thighs.

Her hips undulate with need at the feel of his hot breath on her. She squirms with frustration as his palms travel over her thighs, fingertips reaching the crease where her thighs meet her pelvis. Eyes closed, her head drops back as his touch reaches her labia and he opens her gently, his breath hot. She tries to move forward but his hands are on her hips, holding her still.

She cries out as his hot tongue engulfs her clit—and retreats. Once, twice, too slowly. She is impatient to explode against his tongue. Thrice and she is gasping, writhing. He doesn't pull away. His tongue plays against her clit, the heels of his hands steadying her against the wall and preventing her from sinking to the floor. The elongated pleasure is thrilling but unsatisfying, the pinnacle somehow just out of reach.

She sobs with frustration as his mouth pulls away, but he guides her pleasure-weakened body to the bench. She lays back, lazy with fatigue, and watches with her cheek resting on the mat as he steps out of his pants and his erection springs free. The sight of him fully naked is a shock. The finely-honed physique he'd concealed, the glorious muscles hidden beneath loose silk, are on full display. His beautiful cock.

She reaches out to him, impatient. She needs the final release that is just beyond her grasp. She wants him inside her, thrusting hard, his hips pummelling hers. He shakes his head and she drops her hands to rest on her belly, and he rewards her by lowering himself between her open legs. He moves over her, smooth as when he was fighting, and rests on one elbow to brush back the hair that sticks to her moist skin, as if he's soothing a skittish animal. Kalika holds still, willing to submit for the sake of release.

When he enters her, it is not hard and fast as she craves, but slowly, gently. When she lifts her hips impatiently, he stops moving. It's not until she relaxes beneath him that he resumes, torturing her with the slow slide of his cock inside her, pausing when he is embedded.

Unhurried, he pulls out and she wants to scream with frustration, the pleasure-swollen flesh of her passage tormented by the slow movement, out and then deep again. On the next slide out, her orgasm hovers like a sneeze, teasing her with the promise of release.

'Kalika,' he whispers in her ear, and thrusts, hard and firm, just as her pleasure explodes around him. Any thoughts evaporate and she is pure sensation, quivering, crying out with each quickening thrust. The pleasure doesn't abate as it does when she pleasures herself, but the fullness of him, deep inside her, tethers her orgasm deep inside her.

His thrusts become erratic and he arches back, his body hard as steel from fingertip to toes. She watches his face, a mask of focused concentration and his eyes snap open, scorching her with his intensity. He is pulsing, jerking inside her.

THE NEXT NIGHT Kalika takes more hits than she's used to, distracted by memories of night before. She can picture the moments clearly: the first time she saw Hiro, deceptively lean in his white robe; the first time she glimpsed his beautiful body; the first time he introduced her to the pleasure of his chains; and later, when he'd coaxed ecstasy from her body with his slow, gentle lovemaking.

She hadn't recognised the woman who lay beneath his lean, sinuous body, who had submitted and found joy not in combat, but in tenderness.

She smiles. He's promised to call her later tonight and she looks forward to learning all she can about him. But most of all she wants to know when they can meet again. When she can feel him, silk covered steel, inside her.

The change room is as hot and damp as ever. She showers quickly, drying off and dressing quickly so she will be home when he calls.

She pauses. Something is out of place. She scans the room and registers the patch of white on the central change bench. Hiro's robe? She doesn't dare to hope, but glides closer, senses alert for a practical joke put here by one of the boys. But no, it's not a robe. It's a bunch of flowers. White daisies. She gasps and picks them up, holding them to her chest, an unfamiliar thrill filling her. No one has ever bought her flowers before. She would have thrown them away if they had.

Hiro? She spins around, searching the shadows. Is he here?

'Kalika.' A voice from the corner, and a patch of darker shadow.

'Yes. Hiro?'

He steps out, dressed in slim black jeans and a fitted black t-shirt.

Her stomach clenches with desire at the sight of him, lean muscle wrapped tightly in shadows.

'Will you have dinner with me?'

Joy swells in her chest and she can't control a smile of elation. By acquiescing, she will be the winner.

'I would love that. Oh, and you can call me Daisy.'

The Chain Ball

BY EMMA LEA

NERVES BUBBLED IN MY VEINS, causing my skin to tingle and prickle. I ran my hands down the short black dress, tugging it a little lower in an attempt to lengthen it without exposing too much at the neckline. I grimaced at the lumps and bumps I encountered along the way; those had certainly not been there last time I wore this dress. In the two years since the last Chain Ball, a lot had changed in me and my life. I was not the same witch, and that wasn't altogether a bad thing.

A flash of red caught my eye. I turned and crossed to the door where the red tie was tossed casually over the door knob and my fingers itched to touch the silky fabric. Would it still be there in the morning? Or would everything change after tonight? I wanted to linger and soak up the happy memories that infused the air like perfume, but not going wouldn't protect the idyll we had created. I was only prolonging the inevitable.

With a sigh and a final check for baby spit, I left my bedroom and walked down the stairs. I held on to the banister, not trusting the watery feeling in my knees.

Martha, my very human friend and babysitter for the night, whistled when she saw me. I grinned tremulously and did a little pirouette to show off my dress.

'Oh wow, Xanthe. You look gorgeous.'

I let out the breath I had been holding and tried to ignore the blush that heated my cheeks. 'Thanks,' I said. I ran my hands over my dress again and then lifted my trembling fingers to pat at my hair, feeling for any strands that might be out of place.

Martha hitched Polly higher on her hip. 'Doesn't Mummy look pretty?' she said to my blonde-haired, blue-eyed daughter.

Polly grinned and made a cute baby noise as I kissed her cheek. She was the light of my life and I wouldn't give her up for anything.

'Are you meeting Heath there?' Martha asked.

I swallowed and tried to appear normal. Martha wouldn't understand that Heath may not be coming home again after tonight. I was having trouble understanding it myself and I had grown up knowing the law.

I nodded and ran my hand over Polly's soft curls once more. She would one day grow up and attend her own Chain Ball. It seemed so far away and yet I knew it would be here within a blink of an eye.

I took a deep breath. I couldn't procrastinate any longer. Tonight would determine the future for my little family and there was nothing I could do to stop it.

'Okay. I'm off.'

Martha walked me to the door and waved as I drove away.

My stomach tumbled and fluttered uncomfortably as I drove to the fancy hotel where the Chain Ball was being held. I could remember when this was fun, when I couldn't wait to find out who I was linked with. But tonight all I felt was dread.

I trusted the Council of Witches—honestly, I did. Logically I knew why we did this, but in my heart the fear was real. Before Polly, it was all fun and games; but now things were different. Being responsible for a small witch had changed my life and my priorities.

I forced myself to exhale and rolled my shoulders in an attempt to loosen the tight muscles in my neck. It wasn't anything tangible that determined who I would be linked with tonight—it didn't matter what I looked like or how successful I was. The linking was decided by the magic and wasn't that what I was really afraid of? What if the magic chose someone other than Heath?

I took another deep, calming breath before walking up the grand hotel stairs and into the lush building. The sign welcoming guests to the Chain Ball stood off to one side of the reception room. Several witches I recognised congregated around the entrance. I detoured around them to the bathroom and hid in a cubicle.

My hands shook as I reached into my clutch and took out the mask I would wear tonight. It was plain and black to match my dress. There was no need for embellishments; any identifying and non-regulation adornments would be stripped off before I was allowed through the doors anyway. The snug black dress, with its asymmetrical line and one-shoulder design, and the six-inch stilettos on my feet were the same as that of every other female witch that would attend tonight. The men would be similarly dressed in black tuxedos, white shirts, vests and ties, along with their white masks.

And then there were the gold chains that everyone would wear around their wrists.

I reached back into my clutch and took hold of the

single gold link. As I drew it out of the bag, it grew in length and wrapped itself around my left wrist, linking back into itself securely. A tail of six links hung from where the chain joined itself to cuff my wrist and I looked at it with trepidation. What would it yield tonight?

I had been given the link at my very first Chain Ball. It was a rite of passage for all witches—male and female—who had reached the age of independence. The single gold link was always with me, its magic linked to mine. It was imbued with old magic and a powerful talisman that all adult witches carried.

I had been excused from the last two annual Chain Balls because of my pregnancy and then Polly's birth. A year of grace was given to help Polly's father and I bond with her. Tonight was the first one either of us had attended since the incredible night when Polly had been conceived.

I didn't think I was ready to find out what would happen this year.

I heard the door open and the voices of a group of women as they entered. I straightened my dress once again and stepped out of the cubicle. The other witches smiled at me in greeting and I returned their pleasantries as I washed my hands. I checked my reflection in the mirror and tried to ignore my wide, deer-in-headlights stare. The temptation to use a little bit of glamour to hide the rounded curves of my body was strong, but I knew it would be for nothing. If any magic was detected on a witch as she entered the ballroom it would be stripped away. The only magic allowed in the room was contained in the chain. The old magic in the chain couldn't be tampered with and it was that magic alone that would determine the outcome tonight.

DINNER PROGRESSED with the usual pomp and circumstance that accompanied any Council of Witches event, but I was too preoccupied with the coming events to pay attention or do much more than nibble at my food. There was a restless anticipation in the air as the dignitaries droned through their speeches. They seemed to draw them out even knowing that nobody was listening. We were all there for one thing only: the Linking Ceremony.

The Council of Witches believed that only unions sanctioned by the old magic could be maintained. They didn't hold to the feelings of the heart or the fairy tale of true love. That's what the Linking Ceremony and the Chain Ball were all about. It was the piece of magical metal wrapped around my wrist that would determine who would share my bed for the next year, regardless of how I felt about the matter.

It was how I met Polly's father.

To an outsider it might seem barbaric, but my body was still my own. If the chain linked me with someone I didn't want to be with, then I could choose to spend the year unlinked. I only knew of a few witches who had chosen that route because the fact was, the old magic just seemed to know who we should be linked with. I shouldn't be so nervous, but I couldn't help it.

As a young witch I had heard the legends of fated mates. The Council discouraged the formal teaching of what they determined were mere fairy tales, probably so as not to fill young witches' heads with dreams of happily ever after. But there was a chance, however slim, of finding your fated mate during a Linking Ceremony. According to the legends, fated mates would be revealed by two individual links remaining joined after the Linking Ceremony was complete.

I had hoped for that with Heath, but it hadn't turned out that way.

Polly's father was somewhere in the ballroom, although male and female witches had been separated for the duration of the meal. We wouldn't come face-to-face with the men until it was time for the Linking Ceremony.

The speeches finally came to an end and a hush fell over the crowd. The expectation of what was to come settled over us like a soft blanket and my skin tingled with goosebumps. The lights dimmed and I felt my pupils contract. Our supernatural sight was not exactly night vision, but it did help us to see better in the dark than most humans. The darkness of the ballroom was all part of the ceremony intended to keep everyone's identity shrouded until the linking had been completed.

We stood as one and moved towards the dance floor as if choreographed. Soft classical music filled the room and I could feel the press of the old magic as it swirled around us. It was a heady thing and it hung in the air like fragrant mist, adding a dreamlike quality to the whole event. My skin tingled with the strange and yet familiar touch of it, and my natural senses were dulled while my supernatural ones were heightened. It felt nothing like my own magic, but I recognised it as it called to something deep within me.

I felt my nipples peak under my dress and rub against the lace of my bra. My body remembered the last time I had been here—and it yearned to make a similar connection. Or maybe it was the magic preparing me for the man I would take to my bed tonight.

Letting go of my fears, I gave myself over to the old magic and allowed my body to drift. We moved around each other in a dance that we all knew instinctively, although I couldn't remember ever learning it. The soft sound of the chains clinking as we moved was the only thing that could be heard above the music.

I breathed in the scent of aftershave and the men wearing it as our bodies passed one another in the dark. The subtle brush of an arm along mine, the whisper of a breath against my cheek, the hard chest that pressed against my aching breasts had me almost losing my mind until I heard the telltale snick of my chain as it linked with his.

I dragged in a deep breath, my mind swirling. I could feel the hard planes of his body as his unlinked arm wrapped around me and pulled me against him. Soft, full lips brushed mine and I opened them willingly, inviting him in. His tongue swiped across my bottom lip before sliding against mine and I moaned softly as he deepened the kiss. The hands of our linked arms found one another and our fingers entwined, palm to palm.

Relief rushed through me, quickly followed by desire. My worries from earlier were washed away by the need I felt for the man who had been chosen for me by the chain. My unlinked hand burrowed into the short hair at his nape and I pressed myself harder against him, needing to feel every inch of him. The stiff rod of his erection pushed into my belly making me wet with anticipation. His lips broke from mine and I would have protested but then he was kissing my jaw and then my neck. I tilted my head as he made his way lower.

A small gong sounded, indicating that the Linking had been complete, and I gasped. I had forgotten that we were in a room full of people. We parted reluctantly, although our fingers were still woven together and our wrists linked by the chain and the old magic.

We wouldn't see each other's faces or know each other's names until tomorrow, but the anxiety I had felt earlier was completely gone. I trusted the old magic and the chain, and I was suddenly anxious to get on with the rest of the evening.

WE WERE DISMISSED from the ball and, still in darkness, we were ushered to the elevators that would take us to our rooms for the night. I stood close to the man who would be my partner for the next twelve months and felt a tingle along my exposed skin where my arm brushed his. Our hands were still entwined and with each passing minute my need became more acute.

The elevator was silent despite being packed with bodies. The pheromones in the air were thick and almost drugging in their effect. There was no pretence here. We all knew what came next and the shared anticipation heightened the sexual tension. Finally, after what felt like an eternity, the elevator came to a stop and the doors opened.

The corridor was dark with just narrow strip lighting running along the edges of the walls to show us the way. I let myself be led along the hallway until he stopped in front of a door and slid the keycard into the lock. The door opened and he pulled me inside. I didn't have time to even register the room before he had me backed against the closed door and his mouth was on mine in a deep, greedy kiss.

'Name?' he asked, his voice rough.

'Samantha,' I replied, my own voice husky with desire.

We didn't use real names, not until the morning when we were revealed to each other. Samantha was always my code name. I had chosen the name after watching an episode of Bewitched when I was young.

He chuckled against my throat, his warm breath sending goosebumps skittering across my skin. 'Then you can call me Darren.'

I smiled as I tipped my head back and let him nip at the sensitive skin of my throat.

'We should probably discuss birth control,' I managed to say haltingly, trying desperately to keep my head on the logistics before we descended completely into mind-numbing pleasure.

He paused, breathing hard. 'What is your choice?' he asked.

We were all screened for diseases before the ball, so the decision of whether to use a condom was purely about birth control.

I reached out and ran my hand through his fringe and said softly, 'I'd like to try for a baby.'

He sighed and pressed his hard body against mine. 'I would too,' he whispered.

The formalities dispensed with, he captured my lips in long kiss and I melted against him.

'Bedroom,' he said, pulling away but taking me with him as he backed across the floor towards the closed door of what I could only assume was the bedroom.

As soon as we were across the threshold, his hand went to the zipper at my side. The one-shouldered design of the dress meant that it slipped easily from my body without the need for the chain to unlink. He made quick work of my strapless bra and I stood before him in nothing more than my black lace panties and my stilettos.

The men's suits were designed with a hidden seam along the right side that, with a touch of magic, unravelled. I touched the seam and breathed the word into his ear causing him to shiver and the garment fell away. Greedy, I pressed my naked breasts against his chest, my nipples aching to feel the brush of his wiry hair and smooth skin.

His hand burrowed into my hair, pulling the pins that held it in place until it fell around my shoulders in a cloud of blonde curls. I heard his sigh as the soft strands brushed against his skin and he wove his hands through them, tugging my head back so he could kiss me. A tender kiss this time, but no less potent.

The chain clinked and lengthened as he lowered his body to his knees in front of me. He ran his hand down my leg until he reached my shoe and I used his shoulder to balance myself as he lifted my foot and removed the stiletto. He placed a soft kiss on my calf and the inside of my knee before removing the other shoe. He straightened, remaining on his knees, and with my now much shorter height, his head reached my breasts. He cupped them lovingly, his thumbs circling the nipples once, twice and then a third time before his mouth descended on one of them. He sucked it between his lips and pinched the other one. I threw my head back and moaned. He felt so good, his touch sending pleasure along my nerves and making me wet and needy. I burrowed my hands into his hair and held him in place as he lavished my breasts with lips, tongue and teeth.

His hands scraped down my ribs until he found the waistband of my panties. I sucked in a breath as he pulled them down over my hips. He helped me step out of them and then let his hands coast up my legs to my thighs. A slight tremor of worry pierced through the lust as he looked at my nakedness, but when he placed his lips over my sex and his tongue slicked over my slit, every thought fled from my head.

His fingers spread me open as his tongue delved deep

and then swirled around my hard clit. My hands found their way into his hair once again and he hummed against me as I rocked my pelvis against his mouth.

The gold chain caressed my inner thigh as his hand moved and he slid a finger inside me. My inner muscles clenched hungrily around his digit as he slowly withdrew, only to add a second finger as he pressed back inside me.

He kept up his attentions on my clit as he pulsed his fingers inside me, curling them just right in order to touch that spot that had me crying out and my climax rushing unchecked towards me. My hips rocked uncontrolled and he used his other hand to steady me, his fingers digging into the flesh of my bottom to keep me still. He sucked on my clit and pressed his fingers deep as I broke apart, my body convulsing with the rush of the undeniable pleasure his touch had invoked. He caught me as my knees buckled and laid me on the bed.

I felt the mattress dip as he joined me. He had removed his pants and I could feel the hard heat of his erection as he pressed up against my side.

'I love the feel of your skin,' he said as he trailed his fingers across my stomach.

Feeling a little self-conscious as the effects of my orgasm wore off, I sucked in my stomach and his hand stilled.

'Don't do that,' he said, huskily. He leaned down and placed a row of kisses over my soft belly, his tongue swirling around my navel before he lifted his head to look at me.

The room was dark and we both still wore masks, but I could see his blue eyes. He looked at me as though what he saw was beautiful and it unclenched something in my chest. I rolled towards him and cupped his cheek, brushing my thumb along his bottom lip. He closed his eyes at my touch and a rush of emotion flooded me. I leaned forward and swiped my tongue across where my thumb had been. He groaned and opened to me. I kissed him, long and slow and deep and he rocked his hips against me, his hard cock pressing into my belly.

I shifted slightly, not breaking our kiss, and hooked my leg over his hip, allowing my wet pussy to slide over him. He groaned again and thrust his hips, slipping into me and filling me with his hardness. I rocked against him, pulling my mouth from his so I could catch my breath.

He rolled us over so that I was under him and the new position allowed him to slide deeper into me. A sound of pure satisfaction escaped my throat as he held himself deep inside me. There was something magical about being joined with him like this, and not in the metaphoric sense. I could actually feel the magic tingle across my skin, and the clinking of the chain that bound us was like the soft refrain of a long forgotten but much loved song.

He stretched my arms above my head and wound the lengthening chain around my wrists and his. It was a symbolic gesture, but it felt like more. I opened my eyes to look into his and I knew he felt it too. The chain and the old magic might have chosen us to be together, but there was something more binding us. I felt our hearts knit together, not unlike the way the links of our chains had joined. In this moment as he joined us physically and metaphorically, I knew that there was something bigger, something special about the bond we had.

He lowered his mouth to mine as he began to move inside me. The magic that had only tingled along my skin before began to grow to a prickle and then a heat that consumed both of us. I felt the chain tighten around our bound hands.

'Open your eyes,' he growled and I did, not realising I had closed them.

His blue eyes darkened as he looked into mine and I felt like he could see into my very soul. It didn't frighten me. He was laid bare to me as well and I saw the man he was. But I had already known. I had always known.

I wrapped my legs around his hips and bucked up into him, wanting him deeper. He growled again and slammed into me almost making my eyes roll back in my head, but I kept them on his. We were tethered—he and I—and just as the chain had wrapped around our wrists, I could feel our souls entwine in an unbreakable bond. My body pulsed as my orgasm hit me with a force I had never experienced. The room filled with a bright, white light and I felt him stiffen before he came with an explosive climax.

We were suspended like that—our eyes locked, our bodies fused and the both of us surrounded by a pulsing light. Just as suddenly as it had appeared, the light vanished and he collapsed over me. Our hearts beat frantically and the rhythm of his hot breath panting against my neck matched mine.

The chain that bound our wrists unlinked and slithered away leaving just two joined links on the pillow above my head. He rolled us to the side, still buried deep inside me, and pulled me close.

'Xanthe,' he breathed as he kissed me tenderly.

I didn't need to take off his mask to know who he was. I cupped his cheek and smiled.

'Heath,' I whispered as I traced his lips with my thumb. 'I was so worried.'

He kissed my eyelids and then my nose before brushing his lips across mine.

'I wasn't,' he said. 'I knew from the beginning that we were meant to be together.'

I tilted my head up to look at the two links on the pillow. The unusual sight filled me with a joy I couldn't find words for.

'I guess it's official now.'

Heath pulled me close, tucking me under his chin as he caressed my skin with gentle strokes. For weeks I had been fretting that the outcome of tonight would be different, but Heath had held steadfast to his belief in us and his trust in the old magic.

I relaxed against him, relishing the familiar feel of his body against mine. I truly could relax now and I smiled against the crook of his neck where I had burrowed. I could hardly believe that I would never have to attend another Chain Ball. I could barely even comprehend that Heath and I would be together for the rest of our lives. It was almost too good to be true. I tilted my head to again look at the two gold links nestled together on the pillow above us. There was my proof. The old magic had decreed it. Heath and I were fated mates.

'This may seem a little redundant,' Heath whispered. 'But will you marry me?'

I grinned stupidly against his lips as I kissed him.

When we met at the Chain Ball two years ago, my soul had seemed to recognise him from the moment our chains linked. From each day on, I had only fallen more and more in love with him. I loved the way he was with Polly and I loved the way he cared for me. I had been so worried that this Chain Ball would mean I would have to give him up. But with our two links now joined, we were the exception to the rule. The old magic had spoken and we could marry. It was a highly unusual occurrence in our community and bound to be met with envy and suspicion. It was more than I had ever dared to hope for. But we had the proof. An unbreakable chain to symbolise our unbreakable bond.

'How are we going to explain this to our daughter?'

He shrugged. 'I think she'll be okay with it. Especially if we managed to create a little brother or sister for her.'

He brushed his hand protectively over my stomach and my heart almost burst with love for this man. I kissed him.

'Yes,' I murmured against his lips. 'I'll marry you.'

Chained to Her Boss

BY SUZIE JAY

Chapter 1

ABBY STOOD, frozen in the doorway, staring at the muscles in Brett's delicious, naked back. They tensed and relaxed as his arms propelled his body up and down. A trickle of perspiration caught her eye and she watched it trail down his spine to his tight, sexy ass. She held the doorframe for support as his cheeks clenched and released.

Abby took in the scene for a good minute—no, a *great* minute—before finding her voice. She hated to interrupt him and ruin the show, but it had to be done. Regaining composure, she cleared her throat and stepped into the room.

'Brett! Get up off that floor. Your phone's lit up like a Christmas tree.' She shoved one hand onto her hip and pointed towards the desk with the other.

'Ninety-seven, ninety-eight.'

'Brett, for goodness' sake. Your conference call was due to start six minutes ago.' Abby moved further into the office and leaned against his desk. She contemplated picking up the phone and holding it to his ear.

'Ninety-nine, one-hundred.' He pushed himself up from the floor and towered over her. At 6'3, he was a mountain of a man that dwarfed her 5'0 frame.

He regarded her with a raised brow and a twinkle in his piercing green eyes, and she was once again captivated. Reluctantly, painfully even, she forced her gaze from his. If she stared for too long she'd be sucked into the abyss of his charms, never to find her way out. Distance was the smartest option when it came to her boss. He didn't tolerate work place romance, or so she'd heard. But when their gaze met, romance was all she could think about.

'You can't keep people waiting like this. This client's important.'

Brett grabbed a towel and moved towards her, rubbing the material methodically across his body. Her mouth was suddenly dry and the desire to wet her lips was overpowering but also dangerous. She'd no idea what to do if he saw it as an invitation, so she held her jaw tense.

He was seriously encroaching on her personal space though. She willed herself to move away, but was rooted to the spot. He was all around her, the soft scent of his sandalwood cologne enveloping her, lifting her from reality and dropping her gently into a dream. A forbidden dream. When there was no more than a whisper between them, he leaned in, so close his breath was warm on her face.

Oh God! He's going to kiss me. Her head spun and logic and order left her.

Her brain had never let her revel in this fantasy for long. Yet here it was, in front of her, more real than she ever imagined.

Was she brave enough to indulge? Probably not, so why was she considering it? Getting involved with Brett Turner would be a disaster. She'd been warned by enough co-workers to understand that the office was a romance-free zone.

Despite her sternest pep talk, her eyes fluttered closed, her chin tilted upward and she prepared herself for his kiss.

She paused like that, suspended on cloud nine, for what seemed like a lifetime, but the kiss never came and at the sound of Brett clearing his throat, Abby's eyes sprang open. His face was a bare inch from hers, one arm curved around her waist and a quizzical look was plastered across his face.

'You're leaning on my shirt.'

Abby's gaze darted in the direction of his arm and landed on the shirt he'd been wearing earlier. She'd somehow managed to sandwich it between her hip and the edge of the mahogany desk. Heat rose in her cheeks, she could feel it practically setting her ears alight.

'Oh.' She scuffed her sensible shoes across the ground and gazed longingly at a crack in the polished cement, hoping that it was in fact the beginnings of a sinkhole, preparing to crack open and swallow her up.

'You okay, Abby?'

Brett's voice snapped her out of her stupor and she recalled the reason for her presence in his office in the first place. She glanced at his wall clock. Total mortification had taken place in no more than a minute. Trembling, she moved toward the safety of the door.

'*No*, I'm not okay. You're now seven minutes late for your call. *Seven*!'

'You sure that's all? You seem mighty flustered.' A smirk played on his lips. Abby almost wished her employee contract allowed her to hit him with something.

He shrugged his shirt over his broad shoulders, sliding his fingers slowly down the trim to the bottom button. She couldn't prevent her gaze from following his every move, finally landing on the defined ridges of his six-pack.

The image of her own hand on his taut stomach, caressing his skin, tracing around each of those bulges, leaving a trail of goose bumps, caused the need in her to flare. What was it about Brett that had her acting like a love-struck teenager?

'Seven minutes and twenty-one seconds, Brett.' She tapped her foot. She needed him on that phone so she could make her exit. The solitude of the ladies room beckoned her. She was desperate to go and die of embarrassment in peace. 'Why the hell do you walk around the office half naked anyway? It's ridiculously unprofessional. If you got out of bed earlier, you could do your push-ups at home.'

'Are you offering to come and get me out of bed?'

The mention of it delighted her but she mocked distaste with a roll of her eyes. 'There's nothing I'd love more.' She hoped the sarcastic edge to her voice was obvious, because there was total truth in those words that she'd never admit to Brett.

Finally, Brett settled behind his desk and picked up the receiver.

'Morning, gentlemen. Sorry to keep you. Issues with the secretary. It's hard to get good help these days.' He winked at Abby and she scowled back before taking the chance to escape. She slammed the door behind her for good measure.

Chapter 2

Abby spent the next forty minutes in the bathroom, replaying the incident over and over in her mind.

She'd pursed her lips when she thought he was about

to kiss her. Hadn't she? She was certain of it. Surely it wouldn't have been that noticeable. She practiced her face in the mirror and let out a sigh. It was noticeable. Damn the curse of the plump lips. If her lips were thin like her sister's and her mother's she could've gotten away with it.

Turning on the faucet, Abby splashed water on the back of her neck and ran her hands over her blonde hair, that was pulled back into a slick ponytail. The cold water was refreshing and cooled the burn of embarrassment.

She dried her skin with paper towel and wasted no time re-touching her makeup. Generally, she was a sensible, no-frills type of woman. She refused to wear heels because they were bad for women's feet and hurt like hell. She didn't waste money on designer bags; why would she, when she could get a perfectly good handbag for $15 at the outlet store? She dressed professionally, but comfortably, and her hair had never been dyed.

Makeup was her single indulgence. Her mother thought it was a ridiculous waste of money, but, to Abby, the mask it provided was invaluable. Her makeup was the shield of protection that kept her safe. She wished her mother would understand; it would save her washing it off before she walked through the door each night. She shouldn't need to justify herself at twenty-five years of age, but the small inconvenience was easier than dealing with her mother's fussing.

She was careful to never buy expensive brands, not that she could have afforded them anyway. Now that she was the sole bread winner her obligation to her family came first. She did the best she could to support her mother and sister since her mom was injured two years ago. Although her mother helped out with light cooking at home, Abby was pretty much doing it on her own.

That's why she needed this job. Her family counted on

her. What if Brett realised she'd been planning to kiss him and fired her? Part of her would be glad to be put out of her misery, so she didn't have to live with the embarrassment—but then what would she do? They'd be living out of their car within the month. She couldn't do that to her mother, but especially not to her nine-year-old sister.

Squaring her shoulders, she applied an extra layer of deep fuchsia lipstick to give her the strength to leave the bathroom, and then returned to her desk. Her plan would be to deny, deny, deny. And to never make the same mistake again.

Chapter 3

The office was quiet other than the sound of Abby's fingers flying across the keys of her laptop. She'd wasted too much time in the bathroom, but she was so close to finishing she might even pop out and grab a salad to eat at her desk.

Buying lunch wasn't something she'd normally do, but today was a day for breaking her own rules and God knows she had a lot of them. She needed to get away from the office and besides, the leftover tuna pasta her mother had packed smelled a bit funky and she couldn't afford a bout of food poisoning.

A knocking sound shook her concentration. Looking up, she saw Brett standing at the far end of the open office space.

Oh God! She'd hoped to avoid him at least for the rest of the day. A girl could only take so much humiliation within a 24-hour period. Ignoring him, she continued to type but was acutely aware of him moving closer.

The air in the room became thick and seemed to be choking her. She reached out for her bottled water and took a sip, feeling his eyes on her the entire time.

'Abby.' His eyes did a quick flit across the office. 'I need your help with something.'

Her shoulders slumped and she lost the fight to hold in a sigh. 'What is it, Brett? I have work to do.'

'I've ordered something that I need you to help me pick up. It's after work hours, but I'll compensate you.' His tone was urgent.

She stopped typing and stared up at him. 'What's wrong? You're acting weird.'

'This… ahem, package is a little more awkward than I'd first anticipated. I need you to hold it, while I drive.' He positioned himself on the edge of her desk and stared deep into her eyes. 'Please, Abby. I don't know who else to ask.'

'Brett, I can't hang around after work. I have responsibilities. I've told you this.' She waited for his reaction. She was the best employee he had, and she was fully aware that was the only reason she got away with talking to him so bluntly. He needed her as much as she needed this job. He had a sharp mind, but he was flaky; she was a stickler for routine and order, so she had slipped into the role of no-nonsense schoolmarm. It had become a silent understanding between them.

She nagged him. He ignored her. It was their thing.

'Rushing home to your boyfriend?'

Heat rose in her face for the… she'd lost count of how many times that day. 'Not that it's any of your business, but you know I don't have a boyfriend.' He raised his brows. 'I don't have time,' she added quickly.

His eyes softened. 'Why not? I'm not that much of a slave driver that you have no time for a social life. Nine-to-five are pretty standard hours.'

She swallowed hard. The last thing she needed was a deep and meaningful conversation with her boss. Their relationship was complicated as it was. The fact she worked for the man she wanted to make wild, passionate love to was already on the verge of being more than she could stand.

'What's this package and why's it so urgent?' She changed the subject back to business.

'Can you help me?' His eyes seemed to light up and she realised it must be pretty important to him.

'Fiiine.' She dragged the word out. She hated that she couldn't say no to him. 'But I won't make a habit of it. And it better not be drugs.'

Brett let out a laugh. 'You're really funny, you know that? I don't think people see that about you.' He returned to his office and her entire body relaxed.

'There's a lot about me that people don't see,' she mumbled to his retreating back while grabbing her purse. She definitely needed that salad now, or maybe a huge tub of ice-cream.

Chapter 4

'This is why you were acting so strangely? Because the package is a goat?' She shook her head as they pulled up. 'I thought it was because of our kiss misunderstanding.' The words slipped from her lips before she even realised she was speaking out loud. *Shit!*

His gaze darted away from the old country style gate in front of his parked, black BMW and settled on her. The luxury vehicle was out of place amongst the open fields, overhanging trees, and dirt roads. After only a 40-minute drive, it seemed like a different world. A sign that said *farm-house goats* hung from an old signpost, swaying in the breeze to the tune of the unoiled chain.

'Our kiss-understanding?'

She couldn't take him acting all cute about the incident. She wouldn't be able to face him day in and day out unless she cleared the air. Or possibly moved to Mexico without leaving a forwarding address. She placed her head in her hands and pressed her palms against her closed eyes.

'I'm so embarrassed. When you leaned in for your shirt I thought… well, I thought…'

'It's okay,' he interrupted her, but then silence filled the space between them. After a moment, he continued. 'What if I told you, you were right? I wanted to kiss you too, Abby.' His voice changed; it became thick and husky, like one might have if they'd had their sleep disturbed.

She risked a glance at his eyes, trying to read what she saw there. Was it sympathy or honesty staring back at her? Or something else entirely? Like lust.

'I'd say that I think you're heroically trying to save me from embarrassment.'

'I'd say you think too much.' He leaned in and took her face in his hands. Despite the fact she was almost certain he was going to kiss her this time, she kept her eyes open until his lips crushed against hers.

Once the kiss began it was like an out of control train; nothing she had within her could stop her desire from taking over. She leaned over the centre console and inter-locked her fingers behind his neck, pulling him in and deepening their kiss.

His tongue searched for hers, teasing it into his mouth, where he sucked on it gently before releasing it. Her hands travelled up from his neck and tangled in his hair, drawing him even closer. His hands were in her hair too and when it splayed out around her neck, she realised he'd pulled the band from her ponytail, letting it hang free.

Brett groaned and shifted in his seat. She wanted to suggest they go somewhere else, somewhere more comfort-able, but she wasn't in a hurry to break his kiss.

Abby's brain was still trying to think, to be logical, but she couldn't hear anything above the sound of her heart beating wildly. Was this what passion was supposed to feel like or had fate decided to strike her down with a heart attack to teach her a lesson for being so stupid?

Brett never dated women from work, his disinterest—despite the attempts of many women—was legendary and often the hot topic around the water cooler. Yet she threw herself at him, first chance she got. But he wasn't pushing her away. In fact, unless she was very much mistaken, he was as into this kiss, this moment, as she was. How in the world could she stop now? Why should she? She'd dreamed about this, fantasised about it, the idea of this moment had consumed her since she started working for him. She was being handed her most intense fantasy on a silver platter. There was no way she could say no.

Brett's hand fought her organza shirt for a touch of her skin. His fingers glided, warm, against her bare skin, sending a shiver through her. This was really happening.

She squeezed her eyes shut concentrating on the feel of his lips as he dropped kisses along her jaw to her neck, where he nibbled gently, sucking the skin into his mouth before releasing it again. She tilted her head back and let out a moan.

His hand slid higher and cupped her breast, his fingers trailing lightly across her satin bra, and over her erect nipple. He twisted gently and she knew she was completely at his mercy. His gaze locked on hers, questioning, waiting for some sort of permission. She managed a small curl of her lips. With trembling hands, she slowly undid the buttons of her shirt, exposing her cream coloured bra. It was all the invitation he needed.

He immediately unhooked the front clasp and bent his head until his mouth latched around her nipple. He teased her with his tongue, drawing circles around the areola and then sucking it gently into his mouth. He tugged at it, drawing his teeth slightly more urgently across her breast.

Brett's hand dropped to the hem of her skirt where he inched it higher and higher on her thigh, before he trailed two fingers from her knee and up her leg, pausing at the edge of her panties. Gasping, she held her breath, afraid to move and almost more afraid not to.

The waiting was torture and she couldn't stand it any longer. Her breath escaped her lungs in short jagged gasps. Repositioning her hips and arching her back, she wiggled her skirt up higher and spread her legs until her knee pressed into the door handle. He slipped his fingers past the flimsy fabric and pushed into her. The instant his fingers entered her tension built inside of her, like a tightly wound spring, desperate for release. She bucked against the heel of his hand, gently at first, then harder and harder until her need to feel him compelled her.

She reached out, searching for him and her hand landed in his lap. She slid her hand higher until she felt his cock, straining against his trousers, desperate to break free. Even with a sheath of material between them she gasped at the size of him. She fumbled at his zip, managing to inch it down slowly. He swayed his hips, trying to accommodate her, but the car was too small to get his trousers off. Instead she rubbed her palm against the bulge, feeling him get harder and harder until she heard him groan.

His fingers delved deeper and she stretched to accommodate them. With each pulse of her inner muscles he pushed deeper, swirling his fingers inside her. She let him go and gripped the edges of the leather seat squeezing tightly, biting her lip to keep from screaming out. When his thumb came down on her clit and rubbed methodically back and forth, she no longer had control over the sounds escaping her lips and even less control over the strange warmth that washed over her and left her shaking.

Knock, knock, knock.

Someone leaned next to the car, peering into the dark, tinted window.

Abby jumped clear back into her seat and instinctively smoothed her hair as she watched Brett struggle to zip his pants up. She twisted in her seat, yanking at the hem of her skirt until it covered her thighs. Brett swiped his hair back into place before hovering his finger over the button to lower his window.

'Wait,' she gasped, clutching at her shirt with trembling hands.

'Here.' Brett quickly fastened the middle three buttons and tucked a tendril of hair behind her ear before rolling down the window.

'You people here to pick up a goat?' The man dipped his head to look inside the car, his eye's darting around suspiciously.

'You've got to be kid-ding me,' Brett quipped and was met by a blank stare. 'Yes sir, hang on, I'll help you load him in the back. My friend's going to keep hold of the chain from the front seat.'

Chapter 5

'Don't hold him by the collar; grab the chain!' Abby shouted as the baby goat took off down the street, bounding from one neighbouring house to the next.

Brett chased after him, his powerful limbs making the act of running look easy. When they returned, he said, 'I caught him four houses down, munching on the flowers. If Mrs Macbeth caught him eating her prize roses, she'd have him for next Sunday's brunch.'

'That might not be such a bad option,' Abby said. 'Why'd you buy a goat anyway?'

'It's a symbolic gift for my little brother. He wanted a pet and I found out yesterday that he's been awarded most valuable newcomer at his basketball club.'

'And a goat is symbolic because…? Does your brother eat roses too?'

Brett laughed as he dug into his pockets and produced his keys. 'No. GOAT. You know, "Greatest Of All Time". I thought it could be a pet and a sort of personal mascot.'

Abby stared at him as though his hair was on fire. 'Goats seem like a lot of work. Are your parents going to be okay with this inheritance?'

'My brother lives with me. He's ten and I'm pretty much the only father he's ever known.' He looked down at his shoes for a moment before lifting his gaze again. 'I don't come from a great family, Abby. My dad was never in the picture and my mother became an alcoholic when my grandmother died. I've been caring for Jack ever since.'

Abby stared, seeing him for more than she'd ever seen before. He'd always seemed so carefree, so irresponsible, yet he was in almost the same situation as she was. 'I didn't realise. I'm sorry, Brett.'

'I've never really told anyone. But it's okay. We do all right. He's a funny kid. He's staying at a friend's house tonight, so I could orchestrate Operation Gregory the Goat. I'd love for you to meet my brother. Maybe at his game next Saturday, you could help me hand out orange wedges at half time?'

'I… I'd like that.' Did Brett Turner just invite her on a date? A date to meet the most important person in the world to him. An indication he didn't regret what happened in the car. Suddenly the world seemed brighter and the rose in Gregory's mouth redder.

'Oh dear!' She tapped Brett and pointed out the goat, snacking on his second course of roses in as many minutes.

'Lucky he's cute.'

Abby ruffled the tuft of white hair on the goat's head. 'He is pretty cute.'

Brett thrust the chain at her. 'Can you hold him for a second while I get this gate unlocked?'

She sighed. How did she get herself into these situations? Brett was one thing, but a goat? She took the chain and held on tight while Brett wriggled the gate before opening it into a gorgeous manicured garden.

'It's beautiful,' she whispered. She could imagine sitting out here drinking her morning coffee, soaking up the sun. But her daydream was ruined by the goat charging erratically towards the flower beds. She held onto the chain for dear life as the beast dragged her across the lawn. Brett was behind her in an instant, spooking the goat and causing it to double back. It ran around and around in circles, wrapping the chain around their legs.

'Brett, the chain,' Abby called out, but it was too late. It fastened around them, pinning them together, only releasing when Abby fell into a patch of mud with Brett seconds behind, landing on top of her.

They broke into hysterical fits of laughter as the goat stopped and stared at them.

'Hey goat, don't look at us like we're the crazy ones.' Abby giggled.

That was all the invitation Gregory needed as he bound towards them and jumped up, positioning himself on Brett's back. Abby laughed so hard she could barely catch a breath while Brett removed the goat and carefully unwrapped the chain from their legs, mud dripping from the ends of their hair.

Chapter 6

Abby sat on the edge of Brett's bed, wrapped in a towel and still damp from her shower, when he appeared in the doorway. He held out one of his business shirts. 'Will this do while your clothes are drying? I have to warn you, I think the goat might have made a snack of your bra.'

A thought hit her as she stood to accept the shirt. She might actually be getting something she wanted. Everything she'd longed for in life had been put on the back burner to care for her mother and parent her sister. What if, just this once, she didn't wait? What if she took exactly what she wanted, when she wanted it? And she knew without question, she wanted Brett.

She tugged on the towel, letting it drop to the floor. She stood in front of Brett and watched a smile crawl slowly across his face. It was one of the many things that drove her crazy about him. He was so self-assured and confident. Although he made mistakes in the boardroom, she'd never seen him rattled. It was powerful and incredibly sexy, and it was no different now.

Without skipping a beat, he dropped the shirt and closed the space between them in two long strides. He stopped to grab a small foil packet from the bedside drawer before he guided her, naked, back onto his crisp cotton sheets. When he ripped his shirt from his body, Abby didn't take notice of where it landed; she was too busy watching as he stripped off his pants and stood before her in his boxers.

She reached out for him, pulling him on top of her. She tugged at his underwear, shoving it down his legs as his enormous cock sprang free. Wrapping her hand tightly around his length, she slid it slowly up and down. She released her hold on him and ran her hands across his body, splaying her fingers in his chest hair while he slid the contents of the foil packet down over his shaft.

'I want you,' she whispered. 'Now.'

Her legs opened to hug his hips as Brett palmed his cock and rubbed it against the lips of her pussy, sliding it up to tease her clit and down again, threatening to break into her at any moment. Her head spun with desire and she focused on the pulse racing in his neck to keep her from forcing him inside her. She bucked against him, urging him for more, silently begging him for release.

When she finally cried out his name, he plunged his cock into her, hard. She screamed with pleasure, clinging to him. He thrust in and out, getting deeper each time.

Her senses swirled, taking in every inch of him: the feel of his skin rubbing against her bare breasts, the smell of his aftershave now embedded in her memory, and the salty taste of him as she stretched up to suck on his neck.

Aware of Brett's groans growing louder, she let herself go, trusting in him. Letting go of any control she thought she still had.

Her entire body tingled from her toes to the tips of her ears as she climaxed a moment before his cock released, pulsing inside her.

He collapsed beside her, both of them spent, but it only took a moment for his arm to reach out and pull her close, tucking her into the curve of his body. She rested her head on his chest while he stroked her hair back from her face.

They lay there as the sun dipped in the sky. Shadows danced across the walls and, finally, it fell dark.

'I've wanted you for so long, Abby.'

She smiled in the safety of the darkened room. 'What took you so long?'

'I was terrified we wouldn't work out. My business needs you. Hell, *I* need you. The fear of losing you kept me from trying but I couldn't have resisted you forever. After all, I've admired you from the minute I checked your references and found out what you do for your mother and sister.'

'You know about that?'

'Your old boss told me, and despite it all, you've never asked for anything. You've helped me build my business at no extra reward to yourself. You're kind and loyal and did I mention, incredibly sexy?'

Abby's heart was overwhelmed. The most she'd hoped for was one night with Brett but now it seemed he was as crazy about her as she was about him.

'If it wasn't for you deciding you needed to give a goat to your brother, we might never have gotten the nerve.'

'You know… you could say a chain of events brought us together.'

She heard the smile in his voice and despite him not being able to see her, she rolled her eyes.

Club 73

BY FIONA MARSDEN

DEAR MS SMITH,

Your session with our specialist has been booked in at your specified date and time.

Due to the unusual nature of your request, our specialist would appreciate further details around your particular needs. Be assured that any information you pass on will be treated with the utmost care.

Regards

Liv

DEAR LIV,

I appreciate the time you're putting in to make my experience at Club 73 safe and consensual. I know it's not usual to request the use of restraints, but due to my reactions on previous occasions I believe they are my best option for achieving the desired outcome.

Ms Smith

DEAR MS SMITH,

Believe me, restraints are one of the least unusual requests we receive at Club 73. We pride ourselves on maximising the experience of all our special clients whatever their needs. It is the other request that we feel needs deeper consideration. We only ask for specifics to ensure our specialist provides the best possible experience for you.

Best wishes

Liv

THANKS LIV,

You're very reassuring. Previous attempts have been disastrous. I don't seem to be able to relax in that situation. The last time, several years ago, resulted in a broken nose for my date.

Ms Smith

DEAR MS SMITH,

I imagine going back for a second date was not on the cards. ;) I believe we have the right specialist to help you. When you arrive for your appointment, Karl will be waiting for you at the bar in the Discotheque.

Wishing you all the best.

Liv

THANKS LIV,

It's been great. I hope we have a chance to meet sometime. Are you based at Club 73?

Ms Smith

DEAR MS SMITH,
  I'm pleased to have been of service.
  Regards
  Liv

———

THE DECOR at Club 73 had an aura of familiarity to a child brought up listening to disco anthems and surrounded by photographs of her parents during their dating years. All the same, Chelsea Brownleigh-Smith decided to go with her own retro theme: a fifties-style spotted dress with tight bodice and full skirt that accentuated her generous top half and disguised her boyish hips and muscular thighs—the joys of being a phys-ed teacher in a school with a high-profile sports program.

At the entrance to the Discotheque Bar and Grill, she blinked at the swirl of coloured lights and giant glitterball. Only a few tables at the edge of the square dance floor were occupied this early in the evening. The well-lit bar with its sweep of mirrors along the back was empty apart from a bartender and a couple standing at the far end.

A slender blonde in a white satin jumpsuit with shoulder length wavy hair stood facing away from the door, talking to a tall dark man with a shaven head wearing a classic seventies style suit and gold chains at neck and wrist. He certainly looked large enough to be able to control her physically.

But he didn't look like a Karl, a name that conjured up a vague picture of a Nordic skier. Or the gorgeous Spanish guy in that Christmas movie she watched every year. Not that there was anyone in her life like that. She'd been alone for over fifteen years. Chained not to people, but to the past. But that was going to change, for tonight at least.

The blonde turned as Chel approached and something jolted in her chest. The tall slender figure and long hair had suggested a woman, but he was most definitely male. Very young and quite beautiful, in a high cheek-boned, sharp-jawed way. Blue eyes glowed in the flickering lights from the dance floor, framed by pale lashes. The jumpsuit, with its rhinestone sparkle, was open to the waist, baring a smooth, pale gold chest with a hint of abs.

Her eyes tracked down his body to the tight fabric across his thighs and halted. If she'd thought slender meant small, she was way off. The white satin outlined a very substantial package. She dragged her gaze back up to his face and caught a knowing look in those brilliant eyes and a smirk on that sensual mouth.

A slow burn started in her gut and she tightened her abdominals, gripping her handbag with clammy fingers as she came to a halt in front of the two men. Instinctively she looked at the older man. 'Karl?'

He shook his head, indicating the boy beside him before turning away to speak to the bartender. God help her if this was Karl. He looked young enough to be one of her students.

'You're Karl?'

'And you must be Ms Smith.'

She took his outstretched hand automatically, wincing at the sudden heat that rocketed up her arm, singeing her skin and sending warmth up her throat to her face. 'You're so young.'

'Only in years, Ms Smith.'

'How old are you?'

'Twenty-one.'

'I'm twenty-nine. Nearly thirty.'

That gorgeous mouth curled up at the corners. 'An excellent age.'

'Did you know?'

'Of course. I know everything.'

The deep blue of his gaze pierced her, as if he could see into her soul. Perhaps he really did know everything. He would have read her file. Age: twenty-nine. Condition: virgin. But there shouldn't have been much else. Apart from the request for restraints. He would know about that.

'Do you think it's a problem? That I'm older?'

'Is it a problem that I'm younger?'

Suddenly it didn't matter. Something about that direct blue gaze steadied her. 'No, I don't think so.'

She glanced around the room which was starting to fill. 'What do we do now?'

'We can relax and have a drink, maybe dance a little.'

Presumably that was part of the deal. A bit of social interaction and then… Her nerves wouldn't stand it. 'Can't we just get on with it?'

His eyes widened, the gold lashes fluttering and then sweeping lower. 'Of course. It's your choice. Your night.'

He took her hand, in a firm clasp at odds with his almost effeminate appearance. A leather band on his wrist peeped from under the long sleeves of the jumpsuit with a glint of gold metal. They left by a discreet door beyond the bar that opened into a shadowed corridor. A thick carpet silenced their footsteps as they headed for a narrow staircase.

Warmth from his touch permeated her skin, trickling along her nerve endings. Anticipation curled in her gut. This time was different. This time there was no cold chill at the touch of a male hand. No nausea at the pit of her stomach. There had been nothing wrong with the other men she'd dated. But nothing could overcome that feeling of dread when intimacy loomed. She'd given up a long time ago.

At this moment, she felt almost lightheaded.

He stopped and pulled an old-fashioned key out of his pocket, releasing her hand to unlock the door, opening it wide. 'The Chain Room.'

Curious, Chel stepped past him, conscious of the warmth emanating from his body, missing the contact of his touch. The room was large, the wallpaper black with strings of oval shapes in a metallic gold resembling links on a chain. The carpet was also black, but with a pattern of gold chevrons.

The bed dominated the room, an iron four-poster in black enamel. Heavy gold chains wrapped around the posts and the mattress was covered in a spread with the same pattern as the wallpaper, with black satin sheets and pillows. She laughed, a nervous giggle that she tried to stifle. 'I can see why they call it the chain room.'

He didn't respond, his expression serious, but she glimpsed a humorous crinkle at the corner of his eyes. He handed her the key. 'You're in control.'

The metal of the key was warm from his hold and she closed her fingers around it. 'Thank you. Only I'm not sure where to start. You'll have to tell me.'

'My certificate is on the table with the condoms.'

She'd almost forgotten. Aware of him watching, she scrutinised the certificate pronouncing him clear of disease. The name was partially obliterated with black ink. Only 'Karl' was legible. So, it was a real name.

'What next?'

'Perhaps we should undress?'

She so could not strip in front of him.

'The bathroom is behind that screen. There are robes.'

It's like he could read her mind.

The bathroom was a decadent dream of black marble and gold tapware. Erotic images of Karl and herself in the tub, in the shower flashed through her mind. Maybe next time? There would be no next time. This was not a relationship. She was here to get fucked.

Chel rolled the words around her mouth silently. She never swore but thinking about Karl and being fucked by him was sending tingles down her spine and moisture to her core. Maybe she wasn't frigid after all.

She pulled on the smaller of the black satin robes and returned to the main room.

He stood beside the bed, wearing only a pair of flesh-toned jocks and the leather wrist bands she'd seen earlier. He was barefooted, and she noticed similar bands around his ankles with gold rings embedded into the leather. As she watched, he stripped off his underwear and hooked one of the chains on the bottom bedpost to one anklet.

She sucked in a breath, avoiding staring at his manhood. It seemed to have grown since he released it from bondage. 'Why are you doing that? I thought… I asked that I be restrained. In case I hurt someone.'

He scrambled onto the bed with all the casual grace of his youth. His eyes lifted to meet hers. 'Restraints might not work for you. I think you'll find this more comfortable.' He attached a chain to his other ankle.

'What did Liv tell you?' A vague anger stirred, tightening her throat. 'I thought what I told her was confidential.'

'I know only what's necessary to ensure a safe and consensual experience for you. Chaining you to the bed might induce fear and you need to be relaxed. In control.'

He sounded like a psychiatrist rather than a twenty-one-year-old… what was he anyway? The word prostitute hadn't been mentioned. But she was paying for sex.

He sat on the bed, his legs splayed. She couldn't help looking at his… penis. It seemed disproportionately large considering his lean, almost slender physique. Chained to the bed. Oh god oh god oh god. This was not what she expected.

His brows rose, his lips curved in a wry smile. 'I'm going to need a little help here.'

He waved his arms, the gold rings glinting in the light from the wall brackets.

'I thought it would be me.' That she would lie there and someone would take her virginity and it would be done. Finished.

He looped a chain over his wrist one handed, clipping it in place. 'And make me do all the work. That isn't much fun.'

Curiosity surged. 'Doesn't it bother you?'

'Bother me? I'm not being coerced. I asked for the job.'

'Do they put it out for tender?' The thought of several strangers she would never meet, reading her file, left her feeling exposed.

'Oh no, I happened to be in the office.'

He chose it? She looked at his youthful face, the beautiful lean body. 'Why would you want this job?'

His blue eyes glowed at her. 'Why not?' He waved the last chain at her. 'The night is young, but you might want to make a move.'

Heat washed over her face. He probably wanted to get it over with. She stepped forward and reached for the chain. His hand gripped her wrist.

'I'm not in a hurry, Ms Smith.'

'Call me Chel.' She swallowed a lump in her throat. Why had she done that? She'd done the whole Ms Smith thing to be anonymous.

'Don't worry, Chel. I won't take advantage.'

Keeping her eyes averted from his naked body, she

looped the chain through the links and snapped it closed. 'Are you comfortable?'

'Yes. Now you need to shorten the chains.'

Startled by the brisk order, she looked at him, meeting his eyes. The warmth in them seeped into her soul, melting her fear. 'How do I do that?'

'A single winding lever halfway along the side of the bed.'

She found it and gave it a couple of turns.

Karl lay back on the bed, spread out like a tasty morsel for her delectation. She wanted to lick all that golden skin. From the heated look in his eyes, he could read her thoughts. 'I'm all yours, Ms Smith.'

Where to start? The pale golden gleam of his skin showed in stark contrast to the black and brassy gold of the spread.

'Touch me, Chel.'

His soft voice soothed her nerves.

'Anywhere?'

He lifted his hips and his erect penis waggled, the cheeky action reminding her of his youth. 'It's your night. Your fantasy. My cock is at your disposal. Along with the rest of me.'

Cock. Such a delicious word. She heard it all the time on the sportsgrounds, but there was something illicit about it in the intimacy of the bedroom. 'May I start with your cock?'

She reached out a tentative finger and stroked down the long shaft. It jumped, swelling at the slight touch. He was uncircumcised, and she wrapped her thumb and fore-finger around the tip to drag the foreskin down. The bulbous end was pink and shining, a bead of moisture at the tip.

Something strange was happening deep in her gut. A

throbbing pulse and an ache. The slickness she'd noticed in the bathroom was back, chafing her thighs. She released his penis, conscious of the warm blue of his gaze. 'Maybe I'll start somewhere else. I've never touched a man like this.' Not sexually. She was trained in massage for sporting injuries, but that was an entirely different ball game.

She stifled another giggle, glancing at his balls, tucked neatly at the base of his erection. He had a nest of pale hair trailing towards his penis, but the ballsack was clean and smooth.

'Share the joke?'

Shaking her head, she climbed onto the bed, clambering over his leg to sit in the triangle formed by his outstretched legs. 'I've just realised I spend too much time with adolescent males. My sense of humour is definitely juvenile.'

'You should feel right at home.'

She stared along the length of his torso, to his head, propped on a black satin pillow, the blond curls spread like a halo around his face. 'I wouldn't feel so comfortable with them.'

'Do you feel comfortable?'

It took a moment to process the question. 'I think I do. At first, when I saw you, I was worried about how young you looked. That would be too weird, considering my job. But you don't seem like them at all. I wouldn't have expected three or four years to make such a difference.'

'I told you I was only young in years.' There was a quirk to his mouth, but a darkness in his eyes that revealed some pain she couldn't identify and wouldn't dare ask about.

She stroked up his calf, ruffling the hairs. They were paler than his skin, bleached by the same sun that had turned his skin to a light gold. His thighs were smoother, the hair tapering off at the creamy skin that hadn't seen the sun as often. She moved to kneel between his thighs, careful not to lean too close and brush against his erection. She could see fine hairs, barely visible on his torso. His nipples were hard flat disks in a dull rose, almost the same pink as his mouth.

He watched, his expression hard to read.

Colour washed over his face as she flicked a nipple, the tiny bud leaping to attention. 'Is this all right?'

He shrugged, the movement rattling the chains. 'I'm good.'

She caught herself smiling as she tracked the dip between his pecs down over the slightly ridged abs. 'I think you're right. Do we really need the chains?'

'This time.'

As if there would be another? She darted a glance at his face, encouraged by the intensity of his gaze. 'I feel strange being free with you tied up.'

'I'm used to it.'

'You do it often?'

He expelled a breath as her fingers went lower on his abdomen. The muscles rippled under the skin. 'I have done. In the past.'

'Do you like it?'

'Not usually.' She wrapped her fingers around his penis and he grunted. 'But this is different.'

'Why?'

'I chose it.'

Her grip tightened a fraction and she could feel the jerk that tensed his whole body. 'Did I hurt you?'

A low chuckle released the tension. 'No. On the contrary.'

'You like this?'

'I like you touching me.'

'I'm ready for your cock.' She liked saying that to him. Liked the light that sparked in his eyes when she said it. 'Should I put the condom on?'

'It's your choice. We're disease free. You could use it for contraception if needed. Otherwise, I'm good to go bareback.'

'Maybe later.' She dipped her head, running her tongue along the large vein on his penis. He groaned in a low tone. 'Karl? How do you feel about children?'

'Children? What the hell kind of question is that?'

'That's why I'm doing this. Because I want children eventually. The sex is kind of prerequisite.' She dropped down again to take the head of his shaft into her mouth.

'That's nice. The kids thing. But what you're doing is extra nice.'

She focused on the taste and texture, listening for his responses, learning what he liked. He liked her to flick the tip with her tongue. He liked her to take him in deep until she almost retched. He liked when she cupped his balls and kneaded them while sucking on his cock. He moaned and squirmed under her touch and finally begged her to stop.

'I'm going to come if you don't hold off, Chel.'

'Cock.'

His brows rose and dipped. 'That would be my cock, yes.'

'I just like saying it. I've never said it out loud before tonight. Or fuck. The boys at school and some of the girls say it all the time, but I'm always careful.'

'If I asked you to say something like "I want to fuck your cock," that would be the first time you ever said it out loud.'

She nodded, smiling. 'Do you want me to fuck your cock?'

'I want you to fuck my cock till I come inside you.' His

quirky smile painted a deep groove down one side of his mouth.

She could feel the pulse inside her leap at his words. Fluid trickled down her thighs. Trembling, she shucked out of the robe, letting it pool behind her.

'Shit, you are incredible. Beautiful. Next time I'm going to fucking touch you.'

Flushed with emotions that flowed through her at his words, she shifted forward, straddling his hips. His penis nudged her wet folds and she tilted her pelvis to let it stroke along the seam. She shuddered, sensation shimmering through her skin, clenching the interior muscles.

'Look at me, Chel.'

She focused her gaze, letting the blue of his eyes suck her in. With a slow shift of her thighs, she aligned her body with his, feeling the pressure of him parting her, entering her. It was tight, but bearable, her body still tingling from that first brush of flesh against flesh.

'Relax, baby.'

She could feel his size stretching her, slickness smoothing the way. With a wiggle that made him moan, she settled until he filled her, his balls touching her butt.

Arching back, she revelled in the rub against her internal muscles. 'So good.'

'Ride my cock, show me what you've got.'

Leaning forward, she placed her hands on the pillow each side of his head. 'Is this right for you?'

'Go for it. I'm fucking brilliant.' He nuzzled her breasts, sucking a nipple into his mouth and sending a lightning bolt straight to her core.

She started with a gentle rocking motion, finding her spot, seeking her pleasure. It was right there, somewhere. His lips on her nipple, the feel of him filling her, so damned close. Tilting her pelvis she angled tighter, pulling away and dropping back, feeling the core of her winding up, tightening and flexing, swallowing the hard length of his cock. She hardly knew when he started to move in response, his movements sharpening hers, pushing him deeper, harder, touching the very heart of her.

Her heart pounded, fast and furious, matching the pulse between her thighs. Sweat pooled between them and he released her breast.

'Look at me. I want you to see me.'

His face was taut, it's beauty attenuated by the stretch of skin over cheeks and jaw, but it was in his eyes that she found what she searched for, a connection so long denied. Since the attack that had killed her parents and frozen her heart, leaving her body hard and cold and unreceptive. He knew, somehow he knew, told by the one person she shared it with: Liv. Like a third person, the heart between them making them whole.

Her body quivered, control lost as she shuddered and rocked, her legs weak and useless. The roar of blood through her veins, the clock-wound spring in her womb broken, echoed by his release, sending her beyond space and time and reality, drawn back only through the intensity of blue eyes, deep as the ocean, wide as the sky.

'LET ME LOOSE.'

Chel struggled into consciousness, hearing his words and fumbling with the chains on his wrist. What had she done? He was nearly ten years younger. This wasn't love. It was sex. Did sex always create that kind of connection?

She flung herself into the bathroom to dress herself, hearing the rattle of chains as he released the bonds.

He'd been right about the restraints. This way was

better. But dangerous. She couldn't have more with him and she wanted more. His deliberate vulnerability had freed her, but for what? Empty years searching for something this strong to replace it. She was broken. A young man like him wouldn't want her. Not for real.

'Chel? What's wrong?'

'I have to go.'

'Why. I was hoping… It was good for you wasn't it?'

'You're too young. You have your life ahead of you. You don't need me.'

'Age is a number, give us a chance.'

Tears blurred her eyes. He stood, slender and beautiful. And loved. And she couldn't reach out and take him. 'I really have to go.'

He took the key from her trembling hand and unlocked the door.

She hesitated, blinking away the tears, trying to read his expression. It was cold as stone, the blue of his eyes somehow muted.

'It's okay, Chel. You're free to go.'

She went.

THE RECEPTION ROOMS of Club 73 looked more like a lawyer's office than a social club. 'I was hoping to see Liv.'

The girl behind the desk opened her eyes wide. 'Do you know him?'

Him? 'I thought Liv was a woman. I've only spoken by email.'

'He rarely comes into the club. Only for business.'

Chel wondered what the hell she was doing here. Making a fool of herself? 'I was hoping to ask a favour. And thank her… him, in person.' She glanced at the door, wondering how to make her escape gracefully. 'But if he isn't here, that's fine. I'll send an email.' Not that he'd answered her last one. It had been a week since that night.

'He's in the office with Adam. I'm sure they won't be long.' The girl waved at one of the leather couches. 'Make yourself comfortable.'

A murmur of voices drew her attention and the receptionist smiled. 'This will be them now.'

The tall dark man she recognised from the other night appeared first, shuffling through a sheaf of documents. 'I think we should be happy with the profits for the first year.' He stopped as he caught sight of Chel and licks of flame swarmed up her cheeks.

He stepped aside, revealing his companion. Karl, not Oliver. In a sleek grey suit that made him look older, a gold tie the only colour apart from his hair, tied up in a manbun, and those ocean blue eyes.

Everyone seemed frozen, until Karl stepped forward. 'Chel. What brings you here?'

'I came to see Liv.' His brows rose and she glimpsed a frown on Adam's face. 'Is that a problem?'

He smiled, but the blue eyes remained wary. 'Not at all. If you'd like to come this way.'

She followed him back down the hallway to the offices, hesitating as he stepped aside to allow her to enter one. An enormous couch in red leather took up one wall.

'Where's Liv?'

'Go inside and I'll introduce you.'

She turned to face him once he shut the door. 'It's you, isn't it?'

'Oliver Karlsson at your service.'

Hunching her shoulders, she turned away. 'What was it all about? Some kind of joke?'

'I didn't find it funny. Fun maybe.'

Hope dawned, warming her chest. 'You found it fun?'

'I found it a lot of things. All good. It was you who decided not to follow up, remember.'

'You're so beautiful, and I'm ordinary. And there's the age difference.'

His hands closed over her arms, his thighs pressing against her bottom. Warming her right through. 'I need to tell you something. You might decide that you don't want anything to do with me. Or you might realise that age is just a number. It's up to you.' His jaw brushed against her cheek, lighting little beacons on her skin. Calling her to respond.

'Tell me then.'

'I'm a very rich man. A lot of people think I must be a tech wizard or something dot com. It's how I'm able to invest in the Club.'

She wished she could see his face, but he resisted her attempts to turn into his arms. 'How did you earn it?'

'As a plaything for rich men. They used me for their pleasure for nearly ten years and I sucked every cent, every dollar I could from them, from their expensive bribes, from their casual gifts of money and clothes and jewellery.'

Pain ripped through her, for him, for the boy he must have been. Only then did her own pain surface. 'And you still do that? That's what the other night was about?'

'Club 73 does not provide services of that nature. Your email was forwarded to me to deal with.' His grip tightened. 'I admit I was intrigued.'

'Someone told me…'

'People hook up here. The rooms are available for members. We don't provide them with partners.'

'So why did you play me along?'

'I told you, I was intrigued.'

She twisted around and he released her. 'By a thirty-year-old virgin?'

'A virgin, yes. The age didn't matter.'

'Why?'

A flush mantled his cheekbones. 'Because I'd never been with a woman. I didn't want to be the inexperienced one. Didn't want comparisons.'

Oh man. 'I don't think that was ever likely to be a problem. You could have had someone your own age or younger.'

'I am not interested in immature children. I... like you.'

'You like me?'

'Your emails. They showed a sense of humour, and kindness.'

'This is what you were looking for in a sexual partner?'

His eyes glowed their deep blue. He reached out and brushed a thumb lightly over her nipple, 'Also someone I found sexually attractive.'

Her body responded to his touch instantly, remembering, wanting. 'You chose me?'

He glanced down and her eyes tracked down to his hips. 'What do you think?'

Yes, he wanted her. Really wanted her. 'What do I call you?'

'I prefer Liv.'

'Liv.' She licked her lips and took a deep breath. 'Would you fuck me?'

'With my cock?' His grin widened and set his eyes sparkling. 'By all means.'

He moved forward, herding her to the couch. His fingers clutched her skirts, lifting them into a bunch at her waist.

Her lacey pants went first, dragged down and

discarded over his shoulder. His nimble fingers dealt with the zip and the dress went as well. He stopped for just a moment, his gaze hot and hungry on her breasts in the lacey bra. 'That has to go.' It went.

He stripped with a facility she envied and her mouth watered at the sight of his cock, swollen and erect against his smooth belly. Almost roughly, he parted her legs, pushing her onto the length of the couch. 'I've been wanting this all week.'

She cried out as he entered her, filling her, filling the empty place inside her, easing the ache. 'I've missed this.'

His eyes sought hers, capturing them in a mesmeric stare that transmitted all the want, all the need, he'd hinted at that first night. 'I want the right to fuck you whenever I need.'

'I have school.'

'We can work out a schedule so I'm busy when you're busy.' He thrust harder, her breasts bouncing. He captured them, one with his hand, pinching the nipple, the other with his mouth.

She panted out her response, 'If we are. Together. I. Can. Work. With. That.'

He lifted his head. 'Sweetheart, you own my cock.'

Sensation flowed around her, the pulse of blood pumping, swirling, roaring as she let go, let herself fly. He followed with a shout, thrusting hard as he pumped his essence into her. Her muscles clenched and she soared, holding tight to his slick skin. Not alone. Not bound by the chains of the past. Together they reached the heights, together they would face the tomorrows.

Melt

BY DAVINA STONE

SNOW. And more snow.

Shit!

Rachel lent forward, her full breasts pressing against the steering-wheel as she squinted up at the rapidly darkening sky. Nothing but swirls of white, moving faster and faster in a frenzied dance as far as the eye could see.

How she wished she'd checked the weather forecast for the Snowy Mountains before she'd left. But there simply hadn't been time, she'd run out of the house in such a panic. If she hadn't, Dylan, her ex, would be breaking the door down by now. Just like last time.

Earlier that day she'd punched her brother's number into her phone and prayed it didn't go to message bank.

Pick up, please Seb, please, please pick up!

On the fifth ring, he did.

'Hi Rach, how's things?' He sounded relaxed. Why was he at that conference in Sydney, when she needed him so badly in Canberra?

Her words tumbled over each other. 'Dylan's threatening me again, Seb. What do I do? You're not here and I don't know where to go.'

'Oh God, not again! Fucking Bastard!' Seb's voice was suddenly angry, then urgent. 'Have you tried Juliet? Or Mick and Anna?'

'No one's answering. Dylan says he'll be here in ten minutes. He says he's going to teach me a lesson I won't forget…' She was gasping, the memories of last time constricting her throat.

Seb's voice strong and firm cut through her terror. 'You have to go to Jed's.'

Jed's! Way past Jindabyne, up in the high country?

See Jed again?

Oh God!

She couldn't speak, her tongue stuck to the roof of her mouth.

'Rachel, did you hear me? Go to Jed's. You'll be safe there. I'll phone him now and tell him you're on your way.'

Finally, she managed to say through parched lips, 'Okay, okay. I'll go to Jed's place.'

THERE WAS BARELY time to shove pyjamas, a toothbrush and a change of undies into an overnight bag.

Fear threatened to overwhelm her on two counts: one, she was afraid of staying and being confronted by Dylan's drug fuelled rage and two, she wasn't prepared to meet Jed again, her brother's best friend, the guy she'd fallen hopelessly in love with years ago and never gotten over. Jed, who had touched her, aroused her like no other man ever had before or after. The man who'd turned as cold as the ice on top of Mount Kosciuszko.

So here she was—driving into the blizzard towards him

and in her rush, she hadn't even considered that the weather might change so suddenly, let alone that she might need snow chains for her tyres. It was still early June and up until today, it had been so mild. Why hadn't she just pulled them from the back of the garage when she threw Dylan's stuff out last month?

And what if it continued snowing like this? Images of her little car buried somewhere between Jindabyne and Thredbo, of being found a frozen corpse days later, brought tears to Rachel's eyes as her knuckles tightened around the steering wheel. Already the tyres were slipping and sliding, losing their grip on the white ribbon of road.

Stay calm, stay calm. Think. You're nearly at Jed's.

Phone him.

If anyone would know what to do he would. The guy had lived here all his life. Raising horses, taming and rehabilitating brumbies. A real-life version of The Man from Snowy River. A sudden image jolted through Rachel's panic, of Jed on horseback, the way his thighs held the flanks of the horse with such power, his strong hands barely needing to touch the reins as he brought each wild and beautiful animal to submission.

The Horse Whisperer of the High Country, people around these parts called him.

And once, long ago, Jed had whispered her name. Once, he'd held her—his hands roaming over her body, caressing her breasts, moving down her belly and lower, into the soft curls and the wetness of her dark cleft, stroking her into surrender until all she could do was cry out his name and arch her body against him, shattered into pieces by her first ever orgasm.

It was still etched into Rachel's memory. As though Jed had branded her like one of his wild horses.

She jumped sharply as the ringtone on her the mobile

trilled on the seat next to her. Looking down she saw the word 'JED' on the screen. Heat flooded her cheeks. Had he known she was thinking about him?

She put her foot on the brakes and slid to a halt. There was no other traffic on the approach road to Jed's 400-acre property. No one else was stupid enough to be out in this weather, so what did it matter if she stopped in the middle of the road? She picked up her phone and pressed the green icon, her blood pounding in her ears.

'Where the fuck are you, Rachel?' Curt, gruff, typical Jed.

Every nerve tingled at his voice even though the words hurt like hell.

'On the approach road to your property. I've just turned off the Alpine Way.'

'Have you got snow chains on?'

She didn't speak. Couldn't. Knowing exactly how Jed would react.

'Rachel? Answer me!'

'No.' She managed weakly.

'For Chrissakes, Rachel. Didn't you check the weather? I'm coming to get you. Don't even try to drive in this.'

Then he was gone. No goodbye. No warmth in his voice. The way he'd been with her ever since that evening. Whenever she'd seen him since, it was as though Jed's brooding eyes looked straight through her. Even if he was coldly polite, Rachel knew she meant less than nothing to him. Did he still think of her as that silly teenager with a huge crush? Still judge her for the way she gave herself so willingly to him when she was seventeen?

Rachel sank miserably into her seat. She closed her eyes and drifted into memories that were so familiar, so painful—like a rerun of a tragic movie she couldn't stop watching over and over again.

The first time she saw Jed was through the lens of her camera. She was just sixteen and her parents hadn't quite given up on her riding career. Secretly she was terrified of horses, even if she never dared say so to her equestrian-obsessed family. Seb was four years her senior and practically lived to ride. He was out competing every weekend.

Rachel's love was photography. She was happy as a lark standing by the side of the arena, clicking away, snapping amazing shots of horses as though in flight, their riders hunched tight against their necks as they jumped the course.

Her camera lens, at the ready on this particular day, framed a young guy about the same age as Seb. He had a body made up of powerful fluid muscles astride a glistening black horse. He was competing at the highest level —taking almost impossible jumps with ease. Rachel lowered her camera and drank him in. He'd won, of course. This guy and his beautiful horse moved as one, totally attuned to each other.

When she'd sidled up to him and Seb afterwards, the guy's dark glinting eyes imprisoned her. She couldn't look away.

'Rach, this is Jed.' Seb grinned as he introduced them.

Jed stood with his hands on his hips and she couldn't help noticing how the taut fabric of his britches showed off strong lean thighs. 'Pleased to meet you, Seb's little sister.' His handsome face curved into the most heart-stopping smile, coal black eyes intensely focused on her face. Then he reached out and took her small hand in his.

As Rachel slid her fingers into his powerful grip, she went into free fall; her life split into two parts right then and there—a before that didn't matter and a future that would never be the same again. Because when he'd imprisoned her with his gaze, Jed also stole her heart.

So she'd tried to get enthusiastic about riding. Just to be with him. Jed laughed at her attempts to canter, spent hours instructing her, let her be his little helper in the stables and on his property up in the high country, where his family had lived for nearly eighty years. And sometimes she would catch Jed gazing at her, those black eyes deep and unfathomable. Only her beating heart and the strange throbbing low down in her belly told her that maybe he felt something too—something raw and dark and inexplicable.

Then one day she fell on a jump. The horse bolted, dragging her along the ground in the stirrup. She must have passed out briefly for the next thing Jed's face was swimming in front of her eyes, his brow furrowed with concern.

'Rachel, are you okay? Speak to me! Rachel!'

'I—I think so,' she responded and then she found herself effortlessly swept up in his arms. She smiled dazedly, her head nestled against Jed's chest listening to his heartbeat, barely able to believe her luck.

The first aider who checked her had told Jed to watch her for signs of concussion. Rachel's parents and Seb were away at an event somewhere near Sydney and had left her in Jed's capable hands that weekend. There was nothing for it but for Jed to take her back to his property, instead of dropping her home at her elderly grandparents. He'd had concussion twice and knew the signs.

But she was fine. Even more so for being in Jed's company, having him light a fire, lend her some of his clothes, cook her spaghetti bolognese, then throw himself easily down on the sofa next to her.

They'd watched a soppy movie; she never remembered what it was. Nor was she sure how what happened next came about, but when it did it seemed so natural. So very, very perfect.

Jed turned to her wordlessly, his eyes burning into hers. As he raised her chin gently between his thumb and fingers, all she could do was stare mesmerised as his face came closer and his lips claimed hers.

It wasn't a gentle kiss. It was a passionate demand that sent her senses reeling. Jed's mouth was hot and hard, his tongue prising her lips open, taking possession of her mouth, sending ripples of delight through her whole body. Rachel's mouth opened up to him on a gasp and his tongue deepened the kiss. Jed groaned, a deep animal sound as their tongues danced, and she revelled in the way he took possession of her body, one hand cupping and kneading her breasts over the thick jumper he'd lent her, the other snaking round and pulling her into him. Every nerve ending in her body pulsed at the hard demand of his erection against her belly. He wanted her, needed her as much as she wanted and needed him, and the realisation drove her senses to boiling point. On sheer instinct she pushed her thigh between Jed's, grinding her hips against him, just wanting there to be no space between them, no clothes, just skin on skin as all her teenage fantasies finally came true.

Jed pulled the jumper roughly over her head and then with shaking hands briefly smoothed back her hair. 'Rachel, God! I. Want. You,' he rasped, before his lips fell on hers again.

'Oh Jed, please…' Rachel whimpered against his mouth, barely knowing what she was asking for as she ripped at the buttons of his shirt, tearing her mouth from his momentarily to drink in his hard pecs and abs with greedy eyes.

Then they were kissing again like crazy things, Jed's fingers releasing her bra and cupping her breasts, her nipples peaking with excruciating pleasure as he rolled them in his fingertips, lighting a blazing trail from her breasts to the bud between her thighs.

All reason gone, she pulled one of Jed's hands away from her breast, and pushed it down low, thrusting his fingers and hers under the loose elastic of the tracksuit pants she was wearing. It didn't matter that she had no experience, she'd seen, read, imagined this enough times. She needed him to touch her.

Now.

Where the fire was burning her up.

And Jed did. His fingers working her into a frenzy, his breath ragged, he gasped out his desire, his amazement at how wet she was for him. 'Rachel, Rachel, Rachel!' Her name was ripped from his lips over and over, as he begged her to come for him.

Arching and bucking as the tension mounted inside her, Rachel wiggled and forced her fingers under the band of his jeans and marvelled at the hot hard length of his erection, her fingers sliding over the moist swollen tip, her hand rhythmically moving up and down the thick shaft. Jed was panting harsh and shallow against her mouth now, moving to her rhythm, both their bodies in perfect harmony, the exquisite sensations mounting in a dance of writhing limbs and slick fast-moving fingers.

And then she peaked. Her head arching back against the sofa cushions, a babble of incomprehensible words falling from her lips as the fireball burst, spreading out in pulsing waves from the throbbing bud of her clitoris, rippling through her whole body, setting light to every part of her from her tingling scalp to her curling toes.

It was like nothing Rachel had ever experienced before in her life and at that same moment Jed cried out harshly, his whole body spasming as he filled her hand with the molten liquid of his orgasm.

She knew then that she was changed forever.

Because Jed had given her wings and flown with her. And now they would always be together no matter what.

Except that didn't happen.

The next moment Jed threw himself off her, buttoning his shirt and hiding his beautiful torso from view, a stain spreading over the crotch of his jeans. The mouth that had kissed her senseless became a tight hard line.

Rachel bit back tears as his words struck her like icy shards. 'That was wrong. All wrong. I shouldn't have let that happen. You're my best mate's little sister, for fuck's sake! Get dressed; I'm taking you to your grandparents.'

Jed had picked up the woollen jumper and thrown it at her. 'Here. Cover yourself up,' he bit out harshly.

The icy shards spread like stealthy winter and stole up Rachel's spine.

After that it had never been the same between them.

Eventually she gave up hoping, stopped trying to hang around when Seb met up with Jed.

She half-heartedly dated other boys, studied photography and started her pet photography business. She met Dylan when photographing his Rottweilers. He'd been so charming, so good looking and she lapped up the attention. He was a software entrepreneur who designed apps. She didn't realise that he had an escalating drug habit until it was too late.

And now she was here, in the snow, waiting for Jed to rescue her from this bloody awful mess she'd gotten herself into.

The guy she'd always loved. The guy who she was sure still despised her.

Still, her pulse ran wild as Jed's headlights beamed through the swirling snowflakes.

JED DROVE towards the silhouette of Rachel's car, already covered in a thick blanket of snow.

Bloody woman! Wasn't it enough that she haunted his dreams? She didn't need to cause him to go out in this infernal weather to rescue her.

As if you didn't want to?

As if your heart didn't lurch back into life when Seb rang and said she was on her way?

He couldn't pretend anymore. Not now that Rachel had finally escaped that jerk he'd watched her date from a distance. The jerk who got in first just as he was about to beg her to forgive him, after he'd been such a fucking idiot to ever let her go.

He was level with her car window now and he pumped the brakes and wound his down, schooling his face into his special Rachel mask. The mask he hid behind. Because she unravelled him, turned him to mush every time he saw her.

He took in how drawn her features were in the twilight. Her always pale skin ashen white, dark shadows under those cornflower blue eyes. But still her beauty punched him in the gut—the soft waves of golden hair pulled back into a makeshift bun, escapee fronds falling in wisps around her face. How he ached to take that soft body into his arms and murmur his true feelings into the curve of her neck.

But he didn't.

He just said curtly, 'Come on, grab your stuff and climb in. We'll pick your car up when the weather improves.'

Then Rachel was sitting next to him, shivering, her overnight bag clutched to her breasts. She stared stonily ahead. Jed glanced at the soft plumpness of her lips, her slightly tip-tilted nose, and his insides clenched with longing.

They drove at a snail's pace in silence, but before long Jed realised the snow was now too thick even for his snow chains. They would have to stop at the hut. The little stone building ten kilometres from the main house. There was a makeshift fireplace and wood. An old bed and thick eiderdowns. Probably some tins of food in the cupboard. They'd survive. But would he survive being in that tiny place with Rachel? Sharing the only bed with her?

'We'll only get as far as the hut,' he muttered. 'This weather's closing in. I can't guarantee we'll make it to the homestead and the hut will be a darn sight more comfortable than the car for the night.'

'The hut?' Her voice sounded so small and broken it cut him deep.

'Remember the old stone building at the entrance of the property? It's sometimes used as extra accommodation when I run riding retreats.'

'Oh, I see,' she said flatly.

Soon they were inside the hut, the tension like a silent scream between them. All the things Jed knew he should say, wanted to say, needed to say running like an express train through his head.

Instead he busied himself getting the place in order. Pulling bedding out of the wardrobe. Using what little dry wood there was to make up a fire.

He couldn't bare her standing there, watching him. 'Sit down Rachel,' he said brusquely.

She sank onto one of the rickety chairs at the old table and a little sound escaped her lips. Jed's head shot up to see the tears rolling down her cheeks.

And something broke open inside him.

He went over and knelt down in front of her, clenching

his shaking hands into fists at his side. 'What did the bastard do to you?'

She turned her face away from his gaze, her voice hiccupping on the words when she spoke. 'N—nothing. J— just threats. I left before he got to my place.'

Every muscle and sinew in Jed's body tensed at that, his jaw nearly cracking with anger. He knew that the bastard had hit her before, how she now had a restraining order out on him. Seb had told him everything a month ago.

'I'd kill him,' he muttered thickly.

'What?' Her beautiful eyes met his and he found himself drowning in two dark blue pools.

'I'd kill him if he ever hurt you again.'

He saw her shiver, from fear or cold or something else, he wasn't sure. Then her soft lips turned down and she swiped at the tears on her cheeks with the back of her hand. 'Why would you care?'

Shit.

This was it.

Showdown time.

The snow had muffled every external sound and all Jed could hear was the crackle of the fire, his uneven breathing and Rachel's little sniffs as she stared at her tightly clasped hands in her lap. She was biting her lower lip, her breasts heaving. He sucked in the sharp cold air, exhaled and watched the steam like smoke rising from his lips. It was time. Time for the talk he should have had with Rachel years ago. Fate had finally delivered him the opportunity; he couldn't let it slide like her car in the snow without chains.

'Because you mean too much to me,' he growled.

Rachel's lovely mouth opened in a tiny gasp.

'Jed! I—I don't understand? I thought you hated me since—' she stalled, her lashes shielding her eyes.

'Hated you? I haven't stopped wanting you. Not since that night—' His tongue felt like sandpaper, but he forced out the words, resisting touching her though every part of him wanted to fold her in his arms. 'I was a complete idiot, Rachel. Angry that I let myself get carried away, embarrassed at how much you affected me—how you turned my world upside down. I felt so guilty that I'd taken advantage of you. I had no idea how to handle what I felt and so, yeah, I admit it, I behaved like a complete shit towards you.'

'For ten years?' She sniffed. 'You think that was okay?'

'No, it wasn't okay!' His voice gritty now with self-disgust, Jed flailed around for words. 'I dug myself into a hole so deep I couldn't climb out. Those years when you were at uni in Sydney, when I hardly saw you, drove me insane. And then when I did, I just couldn't seem to break through it. You are so beautiful; every guy was salivating over you. In the end I convinced myself it wouldn't ever work between us. But when you came back to Canberra two years ago I decided, what the hell, what was there to lose? I'd tell you, but by then you'd shacked up with that dickhead Dylan.'

He saw her smile, a tiny little quirk of her lips even though her head was still bent. It gave him sudden courage. 'Tell me what?' she whispered.

'That I love you. Have since the moment I set eyes on you,' he muttered, barely daring to move or breathe. He heard her inhale sharply and saw how her smile deepened. 'Rachel look at me.'

She did, her eyes a swirling vortex of blue passion.

'If you love me, prove it!' Her husky demand knocked him sideways. He gazed at the trembling invitation of her mouth, smelt her intoxicating warmth, soap and sweet skin and the subtle scent of her musky desire and with a groan he grabbed hold of her shoulders and his mouth crushed hers.

Ten years was a long time to hold back.

The way Rachel's lips answered his so urgently told Jed much more than words. As her tongue lashed wet and provocative into his mouth, he hardened like granite. He couldn't wait any longer to make love to her. She moaned as he scooped her out of the chair, still kissing her deeply, and carried her to the bed. The mattress complained as he laid her down and for a second he feasted on the gorgeous curves of body, her golden hair falling out of its confines and splaying like a halo around her shoulders.

How many times had he fantasised about this moment?

Rachel reached up to him, eyes on fire. 'Jed, I want you. Please—'

And that little gesture undid him. He eased himself onto her, feeling her body moulding to his, her softness against the hard fibre of his muscles and his mouth hungrily reclaimed hers—like a man dying of thirst stumbling on an oasis.

Rachel flung her legs around him, her hips grinding against his pulsing erection as she moaned his name.

Jeesh! It would all be over in a second if he didn't stop her in the only way he knew how.

To pleasure her first with his lips and tongue.

Jed pushed up on his forearms, peeled her legs away from him and heard her moan in protest then in invitation as he moved down her body, unbuttoning her shirt and bra, freeing those creamy white orbs, sliding the taut nipples into his mouth one at a time, sucking and flicking his tongue over them until she called out his name and fisted her hands into his hair. He held off with every bit of willpower he possessed, moving lower, his fingers now easing down her leggings and feathering kisses across the soft mound of her stomach, nudging away the lace of her panties.

'Jed, oh-oh-ahhh! Oh, yes, more!'

'Oh yes, my love. This is all for you,' he murmured thickly, barely missing a beat as his mouth slid into the soft blonde curls and then lower, sipping like nectar the wetness in between her trembling thighs and forging deeper, until his tongue circled her tiny erect clitoris.

Rachel was beside herself now, her head thrashing from side to side, her body squirming. Jed clamped his hands firmly around each of her slender thighs to hold her steady. Circling soft but firm over the tight little bud, he let his tongue work its magic faster, pushing two fingers rhythmically inside her, her muscles closing around them as she moaned louder, sensing that her body was so close now as her pelvis pushed deeper into his lapping tongue, then that sudden gush of sweet liquid and her long low cry as she came for him in long pulsing spasms.

Finally Rachel was his. Unconditionally.

Moments later, lips swollen and eyes drunk from her orgasm, she pulled him back up to her and together they ripped off his top, unzipped and rid him of his jeans. Now naked, Jed lowered on to her, melding flesh on flesh.

'You and me together. Please, Jed!' Rachel almost sobbed.

He gritted his teeth and held off a moment. 'Protection?'

'I'm on the pill,' she panted.

Relief flooded through him and she murmured, her lips hot against his mouth, 'Oh my, Jed. I love you so much!' Words deserted him as her warm fingers encased the hard length of his cock and he groaned low in his throat. He knew Rachel's touch so well, even though it had only been the once. How could he ever forget?

She was guiding him to that same dark paradise between her thighs where his tongue and fingers had been moments earlier. Jed could barely hold back as the pulsating warmth engulfed him—but he took his first thrust gentle and slow, wanting so much to prolong this moment, not willing to give himself up to heaven quite yet.

Rachel's internal muscles pulled around him as he sunk deeper and deeper into her. His neck arched involuntarily, every muscle banding as he held still for one more exquisite moment. Then with a harsh curse, Jed's self-control was gone and he was thrusting hard, deep, fast into her, filling her, giving in to the momentum finally, as the urgent need for release built—sensing Rachel was so close again as her body rose to meet his.

'Rachel! God! Rachel!' he cried out with one last carnal thrust as the waves of his orgasm crashed through him. Her answering cries and her body shuddering in answer tipped them both over the edge, transporting them to a place Jed never even knew existed.

Until now.

And then they were spiralling down together into a dark vortex of velvety soft night, arms and legs entwined, their breath slowing in the afterglow.

———

LATER, Rachel lay sated and relaxed in the crook of Jed's arm, tracing little whorls in the soft dark hairs on his chest. She raised her lips and pattered tiny kisses along the beautiful definition of his jaw. Delighting in the scent of him, leather and hay and clean skin slicked lightly with the pungent sweetness of their lovemaking.

Jed wasn't pulling away from her this time, he was right

here, his arms holding her tight. Where he belonged. Where he'd belonged since their very first night together.

Jed bent his head and kissed her softly, and Rachel gave herself totally to the gentle promise of all the things to come.

When his lips released hers, his black eyes were dancing. 'Did I make up for the long drought without me?'

She gave a little pout. 'Oh so modest! As if I was pining!'

'Weren't you?'

'Yes. Desperately. Were you?'

'You bet. Every which way.'

Rachel snuggled her head into Jed's shoulder. 'You know,' she said with a shy little smile. 'I used to have this crazy fantasy of you riding back into my life, whipping your horse to reach me as fast as possible. But in the end, you rescued me in a ute with snow chains.'

'Mmm,' Jed replied, his voice filled with wicked promise. 'Whips and chains. I can't wait to try that combination out with you, my love…'

Alpha In Chains

BY WREN ST CLAIRE

2525 AD on an alien planet

Talon hurried down the corridor, her heart thumping hard. She paused at the doorway to the observation room. Was it true? Had the expedition really found an Alpha? First Officer Kyrion's voice came to her through the door.

'Damn it, we need him!' The familiar sound of her fist slamming into the polished cedar desk of the observation room echoed. Talon cracked the door open, her hand trembling on the handle.

'He's no use to us. His mind is damaged by the isolation.' Medical Officer Barron waved her hand at the glass panel overlooking the cell.

'We've been without an Alpha for decades, how much longer do you think we can last?' Kyrion rounded on Barron, her amber eyes blazing.

'We have to keep looking—' Barron stopped as the door flew open and Hunter Talon strode into the room, her boots tapping on the tiled floor, a pulse beating in her chest.

'Is that him?' Talon went to the glass and stared down into the cell.

'He's mad, Talon,' Barron said wearily. 'We will have to put him down and keep looking.'

Talon put a hand on the glass and stared down at the male in the cell. He was big, which was to be expected. He was Alpha. Alpha's were always big. He stood against the wall of the cell where he was chained, his dark shaggy head turned down. As she watched, his head rose and his eyes shone, dark pits in his harsh, bearded face. His gaze connected with hers. A shudder went through her and heat bloomed in her core. Her heart skipped and thudded and her breath caught in her throat.

He straightened slowly holding her gaze with his. He bared his teeth in a grimace, a white slash in dark facial hair. She leaned against the glass involuntarily. Goddess he was primal. Something dormant in her kicked to life.

'Open the door,' she said.

'What? Didn't you hear me? He's crazy. He'll tear you apart. We already lost three eunuchs bringing him in. The only way to hold him was to tranquilise him.' Barron spoke sharply.

'I said, open the fucking door!' Talon rounded on her.

'But—'

'Don't argue, Barron. Do as she says,' snapped Kyrion.

With a nod to Kyrion, Talon strode out of the observation room and ran down the stone stairs to the cell airlock entrance. Pausing at the entrance, she waited for the click of the locking mechanism controlled from the observation room and pushed the first door open. Her pulse thumped wildly. She swallowed and wiped her sweaty palms on the fabric of her skin-tight pants. She had never seen an Alpha in the flesh until a moment ago and none of her training had prepared her for the impact.

The first door closed behind her as she waited for the second. Her decision to go in there with him was insane— but she knew she had no choice. She patted the gun on her hip reassuringly. He was chained and she had a gun. She didn't want to use it though; she wanted to talk to him. She swallowed again as the second door clicked. The truth was that she wanted to see him, touch him, smell him. Taste him. Fuck, she wanted him. The instinct was over power- ing. The fact he might kill her didn't matter.

She pushed the second door open and stepped into the cell.

He turned his head and stared at her. Her first assess- ment of his size was correct. He was dark skinned and huge, great muscular shoulders and arms, a barrel chest and an abdomen with a six-pack that could cut glass and he was naked. Gloriously naked and beautiful. Her mouth watered. Her sex grew wet just looking at him.

The door closed behind her and she crossed the room to stand against the front wall. Keeping several feet between them. As she stood there, just looking at him, his eyes grew darker, his teeth bared again and he grew rampant. In front of her eyes his penis lengthened and grew engorged, red and stiff as a pole. Rampant desire provoked by her mere presence? Her breath caught in her throat. His muscles flexed, the chains dragged on the stone floor. His body visibly quivered. His jaw clenched. Aggres- sion or desire? Or both? She shuddered, pressing herself back against the wall to resist the imperative to fling herself at him.

She cleared her clogged throat.

'What is your name?'

He glared at her and didn't answer. His hands bunched into fists by his side and he spread his legs as if redistrib- uting his weight. Ready to attack? Would he really kill her?

She shivered, a sliver of terror sliding down her spine. She resisted the urge to pull her gun from its holster. If she showed aggression it might trigger him. That was probably why he had attacked the others. All their training had told them to approach an Alpha with submission, not aggression. If Xede was leading the pack he may have been aggressive, which would explain the carnage.

Her skin felt was hypersensitive. She took a breath and realised she could smell him. A musky, earthy scent that made her body tremble. Her nipples tightened under her shirt and her breasts ached.

'I am Hunter Talon,' she tried again. Her voice was shaky, her knees felt ready to collapse.

'Hunter Talon.' His voice was low husky, as if not used often. At least he could speak and comprehend. Was he really mad?

'I am Blane.'

'Blane.' She tried his name on her tongue and nodded. 'Welcome to Jayson-hyde.' She swallowed. Breathe, Hunter. Breathe.

'Am I a guest or a prisoner?' His eyes ran over her body and she felt the touch of them as if his hands were on her. Goddess. Her breath locked in her throat and she had to fight the urge to move towards him. He was compelling.

How to answer him?

'You killed three eunuchs.'

'I defended myself from attack.' His eyes narrowed. 'What did you expect?'

She licked her lips. 'We, we have been looking for an Alpha for a long time.'

He grunted and lifted his chained arms. 'And this is how you treat me?'

'They thought you were... unstable.'

He looked away a moment and she had the oddest shifting feeling in her chest, as if a pressure had been released.

He turned back to her and she leaned into the wall again, holding her hips still by sheer force of will. Her pelvis ached as his gaze pierced her chest and her pulse went crazy. 'I have been alone for twenty years. I am unstable.' His voice was low and menacing. She shuddered and despite her attempts to clamp down on the sound, a whimper escaped her.

His eyes flashed. His cock bobbed as he moved his weight and tugged experimentally at the chains.

'Come here,' he spoke softly.

She shuddered, trying to resist.

'Come. Here.' He didn't raise his voice, but his will was impossible to deny. She took a shaky step towards him, her eyes locked with his. She should pull the gun from its holster, point it at him. At this range she could hit him exactly where she wanted. Immobilise, but not kill him. Except she couldn't. Something deep in his eyes spoke to her, begged her for understanding, even as his will impelled her do as he commanded.

She took another step. And another. He pulled at the chains experimentally, moving to the limit of the chains. She swallowed, her hands reaching out as she got closer.

'That's enough, Talon.' Officer Kyrion's voice came over the loud speaker. 'Step back and leave the cell.'

Talon looked up and back at the glass above her.

'No. I've got this. I'm okay.' Her heartbeat thumped wildly in her chest, an echo throbbed in her groin a persistent ache that would, must, be satisfied.

A warm callused hand clamp down on her arm and dragged her backwards. Abruptly she was plastered against a hard male body, her senses overwhelmed with musky scent. An arm held her like an iron bar against his body. His breath tickled her ear as he lowered his head and his beard scratched her neck. A soft growl emanated from his throat and reverberated through his chest. Her knees buckled as she hung in his grip helplessly trembling, little shocks of pleasure pulsing through her body.

'Tell them to leave us alone,' he murmured in her ear. She swallowed and opened her eyes with an effort.

'Leave us alone, Kyrion.' Her voice shook.

Talon glanced up at Kyrion, who was plastered to the glass above her. Her eyes were glowing. She gnawed on her lower lip. Barron appeared behind her. Barron's eyes widened and she tried to pull Kyrion back from the glass. Kyrion swung round and hit the medical officer in the jaw. Barron went down and Kyrion disappeared from view.

Blane's hand gripped one of her breasts and Talon closed her eyes with a groan.

His other hand ran down her side to her hip. He moved, rubbing his cock against her bottom, she could feel the heat and hardness of it through the fabric of her pants.

Her hips jerked with the pleasure pulses in her pelvis and she groaned again.

The chains clinked as he moved his hand round to the front of her pants and ripped the fastener open as if it were Velcro. With one hand he yanked her pants down to her knees exposing her sex. She was panting, helpless with aching need.

She was about to be taken by an Alpha. No one of her generation had known an Alpha. There had not been a mating in over four decades.

He grunted in her ear and bit her neck, her pussy twitched and throbbed. His hand cupped her mons, his fingers split her wet folds and she shuddered moaning. No one had prepared her for this. The pleasure seared her brain, nothing had ever felt this good. Her mouth fell open, her tongue laved her lips, her legs shook. She could feel him, shaking too, vibrating with the same need that had her in its grip. This was inevitable, what she was made for, this moment. She arched her back pressing her bottom against his groin, seeking…

His hands grabbed her hips, holding her still as he bent his knees, his magnificent cock slid along her sex, the firm head nudging at her entrance. She shuddered with anticipation. What would it feel like? An Alpha. She swallowed, her breathing shallow and fast. He breathed hard through his nose, she could feel the heat of his body through her shirt as he held her against him. He was so big. She had never been with a male of his size. Never been so over-whelmed by sheer need. He grunted, lifted her and impaled her. The head pierced her, filled her. She gasped, stunned breathless. So big. Pleasure ricocheted through her pelvis towards her sex. With a guttural grunt, he thrust, seating himself fully inside her. She was suspended on his cock, his arms holding her weight as if she were a feather light. Tremors of pleasure flooded her body. His breath on her neck tingled, her skin prickled and those shooting rivulets of pleasure intensified. He thrust holding her body with both hands. He growled in her ear, and grazed her neck with his beard, his lips a soft contrast, then he bit her neck. His teeth sent more tingles along her nerve endings, her whole body pulsed with the pleasure of his thrusts.

THE PLEASURE MADE HIM DIZZY. Never had he imagined in all the years of his isolation it would feel like this, to be buried deep inside a woman's heat, his body suffused with aching desire. He groaned and panted, wrenching at the chains that limited his reach. He wanted this female beneath him. He wanted to fuck her on the floor and the chains were keeping him upright. He wanted to kiss her. Thrust his tongue in her mouth like his cock was in her pussy. He thrust hard, breathing through his nose, snorting with need. His hands gripped her bruisingly tight. Want, need, aching, blinding need to have her under him, his mouth on hers, coursed through his body.

He kept his knees bent and stabilised his weight to keep himself inside her. He breathed. He had waited a long time to find a fertile female—all his life. And these chains were inhibiting what he could do. What he needed to do. Fury boiled up inside him, swamping for a moment the primal imperative to just fuck her to completion.

He roared, bunching his muscles and pulled at the shackles. The plates holding them to the wall shifted. He felt them give. He thrust his hips deep into the female again, and pulled his hands across her body, bunched his muscles and yanked again with another roar, the manacles bit into his flesh but he ignored the pain. The plates gave way with a screeching tear, clanging to the floor, his arms were loose. He growled with satisfaction and pulled her against him, nuzzling her neck and squeezing her breasts. She arched her back, panting and mewling with desire. She was so beautiful, so delicious he wanted to devour her, fuck her, possess her.

He dropped to his knees, taking the female down with him. He pulled out of her, flipped her and yanked at the crotch of her trousers, tearing the fabric so that she could spread her legs for him. She lay on her back staring up at him. Her eyes were huge, fully dilated, her face flushed and riven with desire. She bared her teeth at him and uttered a little growl. His cock twitched his balls ached. His pelvis clenched. Want, aching need swamped him. He panted, fighting to stay in control as he leaned on his hands over her.

He ripped her shirt open and bared her breasts. Perfect round globes. Her nipples jutted up at him, tight pink buds on her golden skin. His cock quivered and ached between them, wanting to be inside her again. The taste of her tight heat, the indescribable pleasure, drove every thought but the need to complete this act of mating from his head. He was born for this. An Alpha's primary function was to mate and protect.

He growled with pleasure at the sight of her fully naked. She was beautiful. He had registered her beauty the moment she stepped up to the glass. And the moment she stepped into the cell his body knew he would, must, have her. She was the one. His body chose her.

He leaned over her and slowly lowered his body to hers, anticipating that tight wet heat again. He trembled. thrust between her open legs and was swamped by bone-searing bliss. He groaned, his back muscles flexing, his buttocks contracting as he pushed deep as he could go. She had been completely ready for him from the first thrust, her body no more able to deny the inevitability of this than his. He lay a moment, gathering his control, tensing his muscles against the overwhelming instinct to drive her into the floor with his violent thrusts.

His mouth came down on her hers and she parted her lips for him. He kissed her, his tongue taking her mouth as his cock mastered her pussy. Her arms came around him, her hands clutched at him, her booted legs covered his naked buttocks as he thrust into her with persistent, hard thrusts.

She writhed under him groaning in her throat, moving her hips with him. He grazed her neck with his teeth, moved his head lower to find her nipples, first one then the other, breathing hard through his nose. Growling in his throat with the pleasure coursing through his body. She arched under him, almost screaming as his teeth clamped on her nipple. She panted, thrashing beneath him. He pushed down to stop her dislodging him and thrust harder, deeper, faster.

His own breath came in near frantic grunting, growling pants as he fucked her towards their mutual climax. She cried out beneath him shaking and shuddering and he flung back his head, thrust deep and hard with a roaring groan, unleashing his seed as the lightening pleasure pain of release took him, shuddering and coursing through his body with coruscating heat. Again and again the paroxysm shook him, injecting great loads of seed into the female below and around him.

He collapsed slowly on top of her. His feet moved, the shackles on his ankles clinking. His thundering pulse steadied, his breathing returned to normal and his senses cleared.

He was still imprisoned by this hyde of females. But they wanted him for their Alpha. This female beneath him was just the first of many who would seek his seed. What did she say their hyde name was? Jayson-hyde?

He lifted his head and looked down at her. Her eyes opened slowly and her legs dropped to the floor. Her eyes cleared and he could see the sense coming back to her brain. The mating was mindless. It took away all reason until its imperative was fulfilled.

He lifted off her, extracting himself with a wince,

getting on his knees, his cock long and red, glistening with their combined moisture, now lay softened on his now loosened ball sack. The smell of their joining was a strong musk in the air between them and the ache in his groin was momentarily satisfied. The floor was hard under his knees and he had mashed her into it with his hard thrusts.

'Are you hurt?' he asked.

She sat up gingerly on her elbows, staring down at her ruined clothing. Her shirt hung off her in shreds, her pants likewise with only the legs tucked in her boots still intact.

She sat up further and he offered her a hand to rise. She got up slowly and muttered something he couldn't catch.

The door opened and the female who had tried to stop them stepped into the cell. She held a gun trained on him.

Instinctively his hackles rose. Sensing something, Talon looked round.

'Kyrion, don't.' She stepped in front him putting herself between him and the gun.

'Step away from him, Talon.'

'No. He won't hurt us if we don't attack him.'

'He attacked you.'

He reached out and shoved Talon behind him.

'Drop the gun, female.' He spoke with command. It had worked with Talon, so he assumed it would work with this one too.

This one was older than Talon. She had amber eyes and skin the colour of burnt honey. She shook her head, continuing to level the gun at him. He frowned, why didn't it work on her?

'His name is Blane. He didn't attack me, Kyrion.' Talon stepped around him. 'He's not mad, Kyrion, just lonely I think.' She glanced back at him.

'If you want me for your Alpha,' he said, glowering at

the gun. 'You had best put that weapon away and unchain me.' He moved his still chained ankles, and swung his now unchained arms, making his point. 'Or I will unchain myself and remove the weapon for you. And I can assure you, female, you won't like it if I do.'

'Kyrion, please.' Talon put out a hand. Slowly Kyrion lowered the weapon, passed it to Talon. Then she lowered herself to her knees and bowed her head. At first, he thought she was submitting to him. But then he realised she was submitting to Talon.

'I cede First Officer post to you, Hunter Talon,' she said in a low voice.

When she lifted her head there were tears on her cheeks and she looked old and tired. As if she had aged decades in mere minutes.

'Kyrion, no.'

The older woman gave a wry smile. 'Did they teach you nothing in school, young one? You have been chosen as first mate of the Alpha. Your rightful position is first officer at his side.'

'I MISSED YOU,' Blane said, running his hands lightly down her sides, heat seared her through the light fabric of the loose gown, his lips traced kisses down her neck.

'I missed you too,' Talon whispered as he pulled her back against him. She had been away visiting other hydes, part of her role as First Officer. As the Alpha, Blane had been busy organising the seedless males into a militia, patrolling the hyde's borders, repelling the creatures that threatened from the jungle at their doorstep, and when called upon to do so, servicing the fertile females with his seed.

The hyde's future was thus assured.

His hand slid down to cover her swelling belly. His touch was gentle, reverent. Very different from the violent raw mating that caused her belly to grow. She leaned against him, a deep satisfaction in her bones. He gave the others his seed out of physical imperative, he returned to her for love; as the other females turned to their seedless mates for love and affection. The first mate bonding was for life. He never spoke of what the others were like and she didn't ask.

She turned in his arms and put hers around his neck. His eyes glowed with affection. She searched them for the lurking shadows of his ordeal, but could detect none. She smiled and surrendered to the touch of his mouth on hers. He kissed her with deep tenderness.

'Let me show you how much I missed you,' he murmured, nuzzling her neck. Picking her up with effortless ease he laid her down on the bed and pulled up her gown. She let him pull it over her head and settled into his arms as his hands slid over her body.

BLANE LISTENED to his own heartbeat and breathing return to normal as the sweat on his skin dried quickly in the heat. He moved to disengage his sated flesh and pull Talon, into his arms for sleep. She nuzzled her head into his chest and sighed with contentment. He lay awake listening to her breathe and marveled at the difference between being with her and the other females. He recalled his manic desire to kiss Talon in that first frenzied mating. That was the difference. From the first it was only her that he wanted—no, needed—to kiss. The others… the rage of lust washed over him when they came to him in heat, needing what only he could give. There was a pleasure-pain in it for him; a mechanical act out of primal imperative. He couldn't control it, but he didn't seek it. They came to him, when they were ready. Just once.

The pleasure and the need, the aching need, came on him only for Talon, his first officer and his mate.

Ties That Bind

BY C L ROSE

'PLEASE MISTRESS CHAINS...' the naked man spread-eagled on the bed begged, his voice thick with desire.

Lost in memories, she stared at the sun disappearing beyond the horizon. The sky was tinted with daubs of pink and orange—it was perfect. Can you see it from your prison my darling? The sunset is all ours. She closed her eyes and pictured him. I hope those bastards aren't hurting you. She wrung her hands. I'll save you, whatever it takes! Metallic clanks diverted her attention back to the hotel room. She turned and left the sunset behind.

With a flick of her shoulders she straightened her spine, replacing the link that kept her bound to her memories, for now. She walked to her client with confidence.

'Did I say you could speak?' She kept her voice low as she trailed a red leather riding crop up along the inside of his leg. His ankle, calf, knee, thigh… his tight scrotum. She leaned over him, her naked breasts grazing his chest as she whispered in his ear. 'Do I need to punish you?'

Silence answered her. She traced a finger along his ear lobe, then leaned in to nip his neck. His wrists and feet were anchored in jingling chain-link spreader bars, which rendered him immobile. It was her preferred form of restraint, her signature. The surrendering of control was a turn-on for all her clients. As it used to be for me. You've taught me well, Justin. She straightened, eyeing him warily and walked to the head of the bed. He wore a black leather blindfold, a rule that she insisted on. She stood back, letting her gaze wander his body. He was lean, muscular, and tanned. A light sheen of perspiration dusted his skin highlighted by the warm light from the sunset. His muscled thighs clenched and unclenched as she stroked them. He was fully aroused, his engorged cock stood upright from a dark thatch of pubic hair. This was just sex —no questions. That suited her and fulfilled her needs.

'You've been very good…' She opened the drawers near the bed removing a small whip. A personal present— handmade to order in Syria. Your favourite, and mine too. She stroked the firm polished tan leather handle, tenderly caressing the nine soft leather thongs as they fell across her fingers. She reached a hand between her legs to find her aching clitoris. Her fingers slipped between her warm folds, slicked across the swollen sensitive nub. Her breath hitched in her throat. She wanted to fuck. To forget her fears. Wanted his large cock deep inside her. Her eyes flicked to her client. He could make her forget her pain for a short time. You're forever in my heart, Justin! She licked her lips and teased his stomach with the leather thongs. Softly she trailed the soft tactile leather across his cock and back again. He shivered but remained silent. These men are nothing—I only want you.

'That's good…' She leaned across, running a slow lick along the veined shaft of his cock just as she'd been taught. At the tip she pushed her tongue into the slit in a teasing half-circle, putting pressure on his frenulum with her hand.

She'd perfected the technique years earlier. You were the best teacher. She licked a small pearl of liquid from the head of his cock. He stayed silent but for heavy breaths that ratchetted with her every touch. The mattress dipped as she climbed on, kneeling so that she could reach his cock. From her midnight blue garter, the only thing she wore, she pulled a silver foil packet, and opened it with her teeth, spitting the corner away. She glanced back to him, his face impassive but flushed.

'Not one sound as I do this…' With excruciating slowness, she rolled the condom down his length, closing her eyes to visualise a different man. She relished the silk skin atop steel-hard muscle. Justin, I love you. She moved back, and slid two fingers deep inside herself, twisting them slowly. She imagined another man touching her, spreading her legs wide, flicking his tongue over her clit before pushing his hard cock deep within her. Blood roared in her ears, as her wanton desire took over.

'I'm going to fuck you now. But. Don't move. Or come. Until I say.' She enunciated each sentence. The man made no sound, but his mouth curved upwards as his tongue dipped out to moisten his lips. I pray this will help bring you home to me…

She straddled his cock, letting him feel her closeness, her damp musky heat. Then, slowly she sank onto his hardness, closing her eyes as her soft walls convulsed against his solid length. Justin, I miss you! I want you! She opened her eyes to see her clients face. Submission. It made her feel powerful. Not lost. Without you, I'm not me… She began to move slowly. His hard shaft penetrated her deeper with each deliberate movement. Her body heated; she ached for release; she throbbed with an intense want to move even faster. She reached a hand down to rub her swollen clit.

'Move now!' she commanded breathlessly. The man arched firmly up, pressing inside her fiercely. The sound of flesh slapping flesh filled the room. He rammed up into her, grunting loudly. Her head fell backwards lost in the breathless carnal rhythm. Justin, I wish it was you! She was beside herself with desire for one person. Justin! His onslaught became harder, urgent against her softness. She rubbed her clit remorselessly, a familiar intensity building deep inside her.

'Come—now!' she screamed. His hard-deep-plunges matched her frenzied pace, she moaned, losing herself. She fell against his chest as her core pulsed around his hardness. Every inch of her skin tightened with sensation. Her clit vibrated as his cock throbbed an everlasting release inside her. He groaned quietly with satisfaction. She couldn't move, her body hummed. Stillness descended, broken only by their heavy breathing. His skin glowed with a golden sheen that matched hers, both flushed from the intensity. For a moment she didn't move, savouring the fullness of his cock inside her. Then, she lifted her leg over him, holding the base of his cock as it fell from inside her. She removed, then disposed of the condom. His chest rose and fell softly as she donned a short blue dressing gown. From the pocket she retrieved a chain with two silver dog tags. She ran her fingers over the etched name and slipped it over her head. With unhurried movements she untied her client. Spread eagled on the white sheets he was very enticing. A perfect specimen. A top military man who preferred to play the sub in bed. His large cock, now limp, was nonetheless notable. She inhaled to centre herself. This was only sex, and he was not the man she wanted. It was all a means to an end. Saving Justin…

'You've got five minutes. After that please dress and leave. If you want another appointment, please message the number you have for me. Then, I will contact you.' She picked up the silver envelope by the bed and left. Two doors down she entered another room and closed the door. With a deep breath she sank to the floor, shaken with emotion. Could she sustain this life? If she wanted to save her husband, it was the only way.

———

'MUM! WHERE ARE MY SCHOOL SHOES?' An impatient voice floated upstairs, interrupting Simone as she applied her make-up.

She sighed. 'Wherever you left them I suppose…' she yelled back. Her ten-year-old daughter, Ellen, never knew where anything was. Her stuff was spread everywhere. 'Actually, are they near the computer?' she called, remembering seeing the Mary-Janes next to the desk.

'Mum?'

Simone startled as her daughter appeared behind her in the mirror.

'God—Ellen you scared me! Are you okay?' She ran a hand over her daughter's hair—worry clutching her chest as she took in Ellen's pale face.

'I had the dream again… about Dad…'

Simone gathered Ellen into her arms. 'Oh sweetheart…'

'What if they're hurting him…' Tears spilled down Ellen's cheeks. 'I want him home with us Mum… it's not fair… can't they just…'

Simone swallowed her own tears and let the lie fall from her lips, to make it easier on Ellen. 'I'm sure he's okay. Just keep praying for him to come home soon.' She knelt and held Ellen's face locking her gaze. 'I promise you, I will do anything—do you hear me—anything, to bring him home safely.' Ellen nodded, sniffing as she wiped her tears.

'I pray every night.'

'I know sweetheart, so do I.' Simone kissed her daughter. 'Are you okay to go to school?' There had been many missed days, but another wasn't going to hurt. Ellen's emotional wellbeing was more important.

'I'm okay.' Ellen smiled bravely and turned to go.

'That's my girl. Do you want me to drive you?'

Ellen shook her head feigning toughness. 'No, I'll get the bus. Thanks, Mum.'

As Ellen left the room, Simone's heart contorted with anguish. No matter what, she wouldn't let it break her; she would stay strong for Ellen, for Justin. They were a unit, a family, forever bound by the links of an invisible chain. Simone heard the back door slam as she left the bedroom.

'Hey, Thor, get out the way, why are you still inside?' she called to the large grey and white flecked American pitbull who lounged across his favourite spot at the top of the stairs. Her mobile began to ring. She grabbed it as she descended behind the large dog, frowning at the unknown number.

'Sergeant Simone Marchesi…'

'Sergeant Marchesi, good morning. This is Colonel John Williams.'

She froze. Top brass didn't ring out of the blue. 'Yes, sir, Colonel?' She stood straight-backed, worried that her shaking legs would crumble if this was bad news. She gripped the chain that held the copy her husband's dog tags along with her own.

'I've got good news about your husband…' She exhaled, unaware that she'd been holding her breath. Relief filled her veins and hope kept her silent. Her heartbeat rocketed inside her chest. 'Long story short… We have managed to secure his release.'

She screamed, clapping a hand over her mouth. 'What? How…?'

'It's classified—but after a medical check-up, he will be debriefed and then we envisage getting him home to you in the next week.'

'Oh my God! Are you serious?' Her cheeks were wet with tears of joy and relief. She'd all but given up on the military ever being able to locate him. The bastards that held him prisoner moved him so often, no one could get a lock on his whereabouts. Now this! He would be safe. 'Very much, Mrs Marchesi. We are extremely proud of the military effort we undertook to release your husband. He's very lucky to be alive.'

'So, he's… he's all right…?' Her words caught in her throat. It was too broad a question, she knew. It would or could take months to determine his state of mind. But physically?

'We won't know the full picture until his medical check-up, but yes, he seems to be in relatively good health and spirits. He's been asking about you, Sergeant Marchesi.'

'When can I speak to him?' She felt her core flood with anticipation.

'He will have some personal time to call you later today, I believe.'

The Colonel went through a few extra organisational necessities—telling her what time and where to report on the Air Force Base in five days' time. After ending the call, she yelled with jubilation. Justin. Tonight, she could talk to him. Finally, to hear his voice for the first time in over a year. She had to get Ellen and tell her… a soft tune played from within the depths of her handbag. She frowned as it beeped. A message. It was her other work phone. Her back stiffened. It was time to end her after-hours job.

SHE HAD him right where she wanted him. Chained to the foot of the bed, his posture slightly bent, legs spread wide. His cock and balls dangled swaying with an enticing cadence as he breathed in and out. As her final client, she'd chosen him because of his length and girth. And because of the pleasure he'd given her. Along with his discretion. Many had requested her, but she'd wanted it easy. Her centre pulsated. Hand job? Blow job? Either she'd get to taste his cock, feel the firm rounded head against the back of her throat, or she'd have his semen dripping over her breasts, hot and creamy, while her vibrator got her off. She needed to release some of her tension. Because of Justin and his promise. They'd spoken briefly on the phone, which had only increased her want for him. There'd been some mild dirty talk. Not their usual play. Then he'd told her, 'I can't wait to see you smile. I'll be making you smile at least three times a day.'

She couldn't wait, her stomach tumbled with excitement. He was talking about fucking her senseless, bringing her to orgasm as many times as her body could take. Her core tightened at the thought of him and his touch, his taste, their bodies wrapped around each other, the endless pleasure they could give one another. To have him touch her, a husband's touch, the man she truly loved—finally after a year. She almost came just thinking of it.

The chains clanked nearby as her client moved. She straightened, readjusting her stance she traced along his strong spine with her riding crop, pressing it between his ass cheeks and teasing his balls, which retracted at her touch.

'You've been very good.' She slid low between his feet and lay on the carpet looking up appreciatively at his large swollen cock. A black silicone cock ring sat behind his balls keeping him harder longer. She smiled and reached for her vibrator inserting it deep within her wet pussy as she began to pump his cock with her hand. The next cock in her pussy would be her husband's—and his alone forever more.

FLAGS FLUTTERED IN THE BREEZE, a brass band played loudly in a show of national pride. A warm wind crossed the airfield carrying the scents of summer, mown grass and sea breezes. Justin's rescue and now subsequent return had been across all the news channels. The media swarmed in packs outside their house and her place of work in the city. Simone and her daughter had been interviewed by several different reporters on the morning news shows, for magazines and newspapers. The questions had all been of a similar ilk: intrusive, bordering on rude. Asking about their relationship and her memories of Justin. They'd never understand the truth. No one needed to know what went on behind closed doors; they'd invent their own truth anyway.

After Justin's capture she had put all her faith in the military. They will bring him home. They hadn't, so she'd manufactured an opportunity. It was a method that her husband would not frown upon, given his own proclivities, she was sure. She would quickly raise the much needed funds for a rescue. Unfortunately, her self-funded rescue had been an unmitigated disaster. The incorrect intel had sent rescuers in the wrong direction. Instead of celebrating, they had commiserated and regrouped. As of the Colonel's phone call seven days ago she had almost fifty thousand dollars in her savings account. It was now a very healthy holiday account. If that was what Justin wanted. She smiled and held tightly to Ellen's hand, they still needed one more link to complete their chain. He wasn't far away.

A large military aircraft appeared low in the blue sky lining up the runway. She held her breath as it bounced once, then it was down, the brakes screeched in resistance sending an acrid smoke across the airfield. She hugged an arm tightly around Ellen's shoulders. The ten-year-old was crying and Simone realised she was too. A whole year since they'd seen him. Now he was here. Her throat burned with emotion and her stomach twisted with anticipation.

'Will he remember me?' Ellen asked suddenly.

Simone swung her head to Ellen in surprise. She wrapped her arms around her daughter in a fierce unrelenting hug. 'Of course, he will. You're his life, sweetheart, our love.' She locked eyes with her daughter's grey gaze—so like Justin's. 'Do you understand that?' At Ellen's nod, Simone began to breathe again. 'We need to be strong for him, love him as much as we can.'

'I will…' Ellen said with tear-filled eyes.

Simone couldn't speak anymore as a lump of emotion formed in her throat, a foreign feeling of happiness filled her. The aircraft ramp opened agonisingly slowly until it touched the tarmac. Soldiers exited first to form a guard of honour. A drum began to play and then the soldiers all saluted. Then he was there—Justin. His familiar loping movement, slow, but with purpose and reassuringly the same. He'd lost weight but gained muscle. He was pale. A smile spread slowly across his face as he locked his grey gaze with hers. She gasped, swallowing the intense desire that threatened her self-control.

'There he is!' Ellen took off full pelt aiming for her father. Simone stood frozen staring as her daughter launched herself into Justin's arms. They swung in a wide circle, Justin raining kisses all over Ellen. With a cheer Simone took off. Then she was with him—he surrounded her, his arms, his hands in her hair pulling her mouth closer to his. Wrapped in the aroma of soap, perhaps after-shave, she finally felt relief wash over her. Ellen jumped alongside them as he kissed her with such intensity it took her breath away. He pulled away and stared at her, his grey eyes brimmed with tears and something else she couldn't yet read. 'Is it really you?'

She nodded, holding his wet face between her hands. 'Yes. Is it really you?'

He grabbed her again in a fierce hug that almost scared her.

'THANKS, Mum. Yes, we'll be fine. Talk to you tomorrow, Ellen.' Simone waved her parents and Ellen off, watching them until their car was out of sight. She leaned back against the weatherboards of the house under the yellow light of the lamp. Simone closed her eyes relishing the peace and knowledge that now she had Justin to herself. They'd had to do the obligatory welcome home party. Even though they'd only had eyes for each other all night. Now they could take their time, her stomach tumbled with butterflies. Then she recognised the pulse of desire deep inside her that had been building since their kiss earlier.

'Was she okay? With giving us some space?'

Simone jumped. His deep voice sent shivers of pleasure along her spine. He trailed a finger along her shoulder and down her collar bone towards her cleavage. She inhaled with pleasure at his touch, and her clit began to throb in anticipation. Small explosions fluttered across her skin as his fingers stroked her.

'Yes...' Simone exhaled. Ellen knew that her Mum and Dad needed time alone; she was so grown up after everything. 'She didn't want to see us being all, "lovey-dovey".'

He laughed softly. 'I've missed this. I've missed... you.'

She closed her eyes as his hands moved lower cupping her breasts, 'Especially this...' he said leaning in to kiss her. A gentle touch of lips to lips, then he increased the pressure stroking his tongue, tasting her. She sighed giving in to the need for all of him.

He pulled away, his face flushed, a question in his eyes. The angular lines, sharp and handsome, his eyes dark bright with desire as he arched an eyebrow. She smelled whisky on his breath, the musky sweat of his want. She'd waited so long. Nodding she took his hand. 'Come on.' She was high, jubilant to have him back, to play with, to fuck senseless.

At the bottom of the stairs, he stopped.

'Strip,' he commanded with a low voice. She obeyed, lowering her gaze with a sensual smile. Anything you ask, Master. She stripped quickly and then stood straight allowing his gaze to rake across her bare flushed breasts and pebbled dark nipples, lower to the small neatly trimmed dark strip of hair above her pussy. He put a finger under her chin and tilted her head so she could see his lust-filled gaze.

'I'm going to touch you. Make you come. First with my fingers, then with my tongue. Understand?' Simone remained silent—a small, eager smile on her face. He traced a finger along her shoulders and down her breasts where he stopped. She throbbed painfully, her core pulsing with excitement. Her pussy had flooded at his touch. She gazed straight ahead, as his touch brushed her sensitive breasts, trailing along her torso to her hips. She shivered, filled with a carnal desire. 'Maybe you'd like me to be naked too?' he asked. She widened her eyes and cast her gaze to his fingers at the zipper of his jeans. She burned to see him, feel him inside her, taste him... fuck him.

With an unbearable slowness, he stripped his clothes. Confronted, she winced at the thick, long ago healed white lines that criss-crossed his back. Shit, what did they do to you, my beautiful man? She swallowed her tears with difficulty. This had to be about reconnecting, re-learning. She closed her eyes to centre herself. We'll be okay. She heard him move and opened her eyes, allowing them to wander across his sculpted chest and abdomen; she frowned with alarm when she noticed the round red scars across his pecs. He hesitated momentarily. Can he see my panic? She blinked as tears burned her eyes. An urgent love filled her —a want to love him enough to erase all his pain. She brought her gaze back to his grey eyes, tinged with sadness and confusion in their depths. He was shaking, something had shifted. He backed away. She held her arms out to him.

'I don't think I can do this, Bub.'

Simone stepped back, shocked. Our safe word? He crumpled into a ball on the floor. She stood frozen, help-less. This wasn't how it was with them. She was the submissive, he was the dominant. Her mind raced, reason-ing, justifying. Of course he was scared. How could she help him? The answer was obvious, but she couldn't tell him yet. She fell next to him and curled herself around him showering kisses across his cool skin. She held him tightly as he cried, rocking him like a baby, shushing him and letting him release his sadness, his pain. She took it from him, anchoring him to her with her love—forever linked.

———

THE FIRST SMACK hit her in the middle of her shoulders. Then a flurry of kicking pushed her across the floor, the rug burning her bare skin.

'Leave me alone! Fucking leave me alone, you bastards!'

In shock, Simone lay still as he paced the hallway. His gorgeous naked body was ready for a fight, muscles flexing. He fisted his hands and shook them in the air, then crouched in the corner watching her with trepidation. She stood slowly, eyeing him warily, then approached. His uncertain—even fearful—gaze never left hers. She lowered a hand to his shoulder, brushing over his bare skin as she knelt next to him. He gasped, grabbing her hand in a firm hold. Then recognition filled his eyes. He raised his hands to cup her face.

'You're real?' His voice held a tone of disbelief.

'Yes.' Her voice was quiet, shaky. She remembered her question to the Colonel a few days earlier: 'Is he...all right?' Now she knew. Physically, he had lost weight and gained muscle. But mentally, he wasn't the man she used to know, the man she lusted for. She reached for his hands and pulled him to his feet. They moved to sit together on the nearby lounge. She covered them with a throw blanket, wrapped an arm around his shoulder as he leaned his head against her breasts. Her heart ached with love for him.

He spoke tearfully, 'I'm so sorry Simone, they've broken me. I wanted to give you everything, the way we used to be.'

She shushed him and wiped his tears, thinking how to deal, how to tell him? 'It'll be okay, Justin. Our love will get us through.'

He nuzzled against her, his tears sliding across her breasts. 'But our sex life? Without sex, how are we us?'

Simone rubbed a hand along his arm and up into his blond hair. Could she tell him? His breathing slowed as they sat, cocooned. Her clit vibrated at his closeness. She wanted his hands on her, his cock inside her. Patience was needed for him to be ready. Maybe the answer was a fantasy he'd once suggested. It could work if she was in control and he didn't feel threatened. She could make it happen, she had everything they needed to help them to find their way back to each other.

'I've got an idea. It might help you. Us. Get our sex life back. No pressure.' She spoke softly. It was a long shot; she was concerned about his mental resilience and she didn't want to resume her lifestyle without him as part of it. He had to be the central figure, just as he had always been. The key difference was that this time he would be physically present. He raised his head and she recognised a bright questioning hope in his eyes. She smiled tracing his jaw with her finger. 'How would you like to watch?'

HER BREASTS ACHED WITH DESIRE, the nipple clamps had almost brought her undone, as she slid down onto her client's swollen cock. A small rough sound came from the corner, she turned to see Justin with his hand on his own swollen cock pumping it furiously. She smiled tenderly and turned back to her client. 'Move now.' She commanded gasping as he arched upwards filling her completely, thrusting against her G-spot. He reached up and squeezed her swollen breasts, she sighed as the nipple clamps sent shots of pleasure through to her cortex. She reached down to rub her tender clit, screaming out her pleasure as she heard Justin groan his release in the corner shadows.

JUSTIN CLOSED the door behind them and turned to look at her, his eyes filled with renewed sparkle. He slipped his robe off and nodded for her to do the same. She acquiesced and the blue silk slid from her body, pooling like water around her feet. Her skin tingled as he stared at her hungrily.

'You're the most beautiful woman... I just want to...' His voice was quiet, hoarse with desire and promise as he reached for her. 'Come here...' She complied and a tingle raced through her. He pulled her against him, his lips and tongue against her neck as his hands reached to fondle her naked, aching breasts. She purred in pleasure, pushing herself against him, savouring the hardness of his rigid cock. His fingers twisted her nipples into hard peaks and her clit began to thrum with hot pleasure.

She paused, thinking. 'Are you ready for this?' Her voice was thick with want. After two months of voyeurism and counselling, was it time? She reached between their warm bodies to caress his velvet length. He inhaled at her touch. 'What does the counsellor say?' Simone asked breathlessly as she squeezed his cock, gently gliding her palm up and down.

Equally breathless, he pointed at a box on the desk and pressed his cock harder into her hand, trembling. 'I've had this made for you. It should give you my answer.'

Simone glanced at the desk and the exquisite black velvet box. Reluctantly she left him, keeping her gaze rivetted to his. She ran her fingers across the black velvet, then unlatched the clasp. Nestled inside the box was a neck and torso harness made of silver-chain. It glittered under the desk lamp as she fingered the cold links.

'It's beautiful…' Expectantly she tilted her head, eyebrow raised. 'Would you like me to put it on?'

He nodded as he palmed his erection, watching her. His eyes were dark with need, bright with love.

She lifted the cool chain from the box, surprised at its weight. The neck chain slipped easily over her head. Her nipples contracted as the chain touched her skin. A centre chain fell between her breasts, she attached the hip chain at her lower back and stood back. Small soft jingles sounded with each breath she took. Justin's gaze roved over her, longing deep within his eyes. She dared not hope as he slowly paced towards her. Her breath stilled.

'I'm going to make you come hard. First with my fingers, then with my mouth. You'll forget all those other men, then there'll be only me. Forever. You're mine. I love you, Simone.'

She turned her gaze up to his as his fingers parted her wet folds. He began the exquisite lovemaking that she'd yearned for. She needed him to know one thing. She sighed, 'It's always been you, Justin. Those other men were nothing—you're my everything, there's no one else. I love you, always have, always will.' Her words were punctuated with kisses as her desire rose. When his tongue finally slipped across her clit, she screamed his name, ecstatic that he'd finally returned to her.

Final Challenge

BY S.E. WELSH

THE STAFF FLEW at my head—a strike I just managed to avoid with a quick backstep. My counter-strike, a sweep towards his left instep, was met with a block and a laugh. I stumbled. Unfortunately, Raz gave me no quarter, pressing his advantage with a sinister smile.

'Is that the best you've got, Asha?' His eyes burned in triumph, his staff a blur, and I itched to wipe that smug smirk off his face. Not yet, I thought to myself. Don't let him see before the Choosing. I let him press the advantage, feigning growing exhaustion as I swung my quarterstaff with less skill and more instinct. Still, it was enough to have him sporting a few bruises, though no broken bones. Careful Asha. Two more days.

The arena was empty, a condition of the training for Breeders in their final year before being Chosen, and I was glad enough of it. The indignity of being a Breeder was bad enough without being made a spectacle of as well. This was my final training session with Raz and I couldn't be happier. The man made my skin crawl, and not in a good way. He enjoyed any pain he inflicted on me, and the constant hard on he sported after tasting blood was down-right scary. I would not belong to him. I would not.

Unfortunately I didn't think I would have much choice. The man's viciousness made him by far one of the best warriors in barracks, and the bastard had been proven fertile. This gave him the right to battle in the Choosing for a Breeder, and unfortunately I was the prime candidate for his… affections. The man was a sick fuck who liked to break people. Particularly women.

Again, the staff swung at my head and I only just managed to block it with the bracer on my left forearm. My manacles had been cleverly designed, a symbol of both my status and my skills. Not many Breeders were warriors. In fact, there weren't many Breeders at all. Hence my being a hot commodity. Strength was appreciated in our culture, a desirable trait to be passed to offspring, but there was no way I was going to carry this man's spawn.

A great crack across my shoulders sent me sprawling in the sand, pain vibrating from my collarbone to the rest of my body. Shit. The bastard had broken it again. Now I would have to get to the infirmary somehow for Rowan to knit it back together. I could feel Raz draw closer and I almost curled in on myself to avoid the next blow, but that would be cowardly. Instead, I tried to rise but the bastard just put his monstrous combat boot on my back and pushed me down again. A shriek of agony escaped my lips before I could gain control of myself, the white hot pain unbearable.

'You look so pretty there, Asha—broken before me.' I tried to crawl away but he just grabbed my ankles and drew me closer to him, kneeling behind me in the dust. He leaned his body over mine, pushing his erection between my arse cheeks as he ground into me. 'Just think about the fun we are going to have together after the Choosing, even if I do have to share.' He grabbed my chin, twisting it towards him. I saw stars before the world went briefly black. I wish it hadn't. Lucidity came with his teeth around my bottom lip. The metallic taste of blood evidence he had bitten me—the pain in my shoulder eclipsing that of my lip.

'What the fuck do you think you are doing, Raz?' An angry bellow came from the entrance to the arena, and I breathed a sigh of relief. The weight of the maniacal bastard lifted off me smoothly, slowly, Raz giving one final thrust between my cheeks.

'Just concluding our lesson, Edan.' The leer was evident in his tone. I didn't need to see it to shiver in disgust. 'I don't think she is fit for another workout today. You'll just have to take her to the infirmary and reschedule for tomorrow.' He stalked past me, puffs of dust from his passing settling on my sweat soaked face. Through the slits of my eyes I watched the stand-off, Edan refusing to budge so a grinning Raz could pass. 'Careful soldier. You may be a rival in the Choosing, but remember we are in blackout period. Touch me and you are automatically disqualified from the battle.' Edan's hands were clenched into trembling fists, the desire to destroy the bastard so strong it nearly trumped our end goal.

'Edan,' I croaked. That was all it took. His eyes swung back towards me and he automatically moved aside and into the arena, a smirking Raz stalking out behind him.

I attempted to smile as he came closer, but it further split the bite marks, making me wince. 'You aren't looking so hot. We'd better get you to Rowan.' I didn't have the energy to agree, all of it was focused on not screaming as he lifted me into his arms. Unfortunately, I was holding my breath and managed to black out as we left my personal torture chamber.

'Nearly there Asha, it's going to be okay. You're going to be okay. Rowan will put you back together again, good as new. Just keep calm and…' The flood of words washed over me, soothing in its rhythm, calming for the moment. The infirmary was not far from the arena, so I couldn't have been out too long as it was brief moments before the door was opened for us and a scowling Rowan led us into a private room. Only Breeders had the luxury of being treated separately, supposedly to protect them from the masses. What injured men were likely to do was beyond me, but at least it gave us some privacy and time to plan.

'What did you allow him to do to you this time?' Rowan's anger pierced the fog as he injected me with painkillers. They were fast-acting and, almost instantly, I felt relief. Enough that I managed to muster a glare.

'Save it for later brother, she needs—'

'I didn't let him do anything.' My eyes flashed fire. 'You try keeping your skills a secret from that sadistic bastard and see how it turns out.' Edan's hands ran soothingly through my hair. I took a breath to calm myself down, then admitted, 'I was running through the regular patterns, but was maybe a little distracted thinking about the Choosing, so I missed his feint and the bastard took advantage.' As I was speaking, Rowan had cut my combat gear from my body and proceeded to run his hands over me, a light glow surrounding his palms. One of the few good things to come from the nuclear fallout was the enhanced ability to heal. Certain genes mutated and those who were previously Reiki masters found themselves with more substantial skills than they had before. Surface wounds, no problem. Broken bones, no problem. The only things they couldn't fix were those that were present from birth, like genetic disfigurement and, of course, our infertility. Too much damage was also a problem. Despite the increase in skills through generations, those parameters had never changed and it frustrated the healers to no end.

'Took advantage Asha?' Rowan's anger rolled over both of us. 'Your shoulder blades are fractured in three places and your C3 vertebrae also has a hairline fracture. Any closer to your spine and I couldn't have helped you.' I swallowed, immediately understanding the implications. A paraplegic or quadriplegic. All our plans ruined. Tears rolled down my cheeks and Edan made panicky moves to comfort me, a woman's tears his worst nightmare. It made me hiccup-laugh, which calmed the waterworks somewhat as Rowan finished the healing.

'There,' he said in satisfaction. 'How does it feel?'

I rolled my shoulders experimentally. 'Better, but still a little tender.' His smile turned cheeky with his relief, his anger gone as quickly as it came.

'Do you need me to kiss it better?' Hot heat lanced between my thighs as I thought on the last time he had 'kissed it better'. Each Breeder was assigned two breeding partners, one healer and one warrior, to ensure the best possible chance of talented offspring. I already knew I was to be given to Rowan—healers did not have to battle. They were given Breeders in order of strength and Rowan was the strongest healer in decades. He had the right to choose, which would take place before the warriors' battle.

Thoughts were immediately swept away as Rowan's lips fluttered over my shoulder blades, nibbling upwards behind my ears. Edan grabbed hold of my wrists, activating the electromagnetic chains incorporated into my bracers. Immediately they stuck to the sides of the bed and as much as I struggled, they wouldn't budge. I snarled up at him but he just grinned, leaning down to whisper in my ear, 'You know you love being at our mercy.' He was right, but that didn't mean I didn't like to be in charge sometimes.

'Just you wait until I get my own set of chains for you, Edan,' I shot him a wicked grin. 'Then we'll see how much you like being at my mercy.'

'Enough,' said Rowan with a warning nip to my shoulder. He turned my face for a hungry kiss as Edan's fingers traced spirals on my arse. 'No time to play today. The scientists will be checking on you early.'

I grimaced. 'Umm... spare clothes?' I jiggled my arms as best I could while still chained to the bed. 'And a little bit of movement here would be nice.'

Edan released me. 'Have you got a sheet somewhere in here, brother?'

Rowan pulled one from a cupboard and wrapped it around me, swaddling me like a baby before Edan hoisted me into his arms. 'You need my help to get back to your room.' I choked on a laugh, sharing a smile with Rowan. I didn't need anyone's help, and he knew it, but I lay my head on his chest anyway and pretended to be asleep, taking the last bit of comfort I could before I was left alone in my luxurious 'cell'.

All Breeders were caged birds. Our quarters may have been beautiful, but they were no less of a cage because of the electromagnetic field that trapped us in them. Added to this was the daily ritual to check our purity and fertility. It was invasive and degrading, but the government didn't see it that way. They saw themselves as 'saving the human race'. Edan swiped my manacles over the door pad—the only way to open the field aside from the electronic keys the scientists had—and placed me gently on the middle of the king size bed. He left without a word, the medical ward and the arena were the only rooms not under constant surveillance. It wouldn't do to blow our plan now.

An hour later, the door chime rang, alerting me to the imminent arrival of the scientists. With a sigh I moved to the magnetic strips on the wall, arms and legs spread by my electromagnetic chains. Two more days. The thought went on repeat through my head as the team conducted their tests impersonally. This time though, they had an injection to give me before they left. This was outside the norm and was injected directly into my lower abdomen. I grit my teeth against the pain.

'What was that for?'

The man with the needle looked up at me, gaze totally void of any warmth. 'Just drugs to enhance your fertility. We want to ensure conception as soon as possible after the Choosing.' I bit back a snarl, hating the fact it was okay for people to use my body in any way they saw fit, just because I was part of a 5% minority of viable female Breeders. I glared at them as they beat a hasty retreat. None of them liked coming in here, their fear of a warrior making me the only female who had to be chained during the examinations. After I had rendered three scientists and a guard unconscious the first time they came to examine me, electromagnetic chains had become standard operating procedure. I both loved and hated my bracers.

The field around the magnetic strip and my manacles dropped abruptly as they exited. Leaving me free to return to my bed. I sighed, curling up under the soft doona, and sang myself to sleep as I had every night since I was thirteen and brought to this place. Tomorrow was the last day of this existence. I could hardly wait.

———

MY EYELIDS SPRANG open as I sent a panicked look at the alarm clock. 5:59. One minute before the alarm was due to go off. I jumped out of bed and raced to get dressed, eager to start my final training session before tomorrow's Choosing. At exactly 6:15 Edan opened the force-field, a scientist's swipe card in his hand. He nodded for me to follow him. We made our way to the arena where he left me to grab our weaponry. Edan emerged from the armoury with a devilish grin on his face and arms behind his back, which in turn had me grinning. 'What are you so happy about? Got some new torture devices?' His smile slid from his face and the new gravity of his features forced me to take this seriously.

'I know this was supposed to be a rest day,' he began nervously. 'But after yesterday's drama you were in no shape to train, and you need it.' His feet shuffled in the sand and it made me smile inwardly. He coughed. 'I have a present for you.' With a flourish he pulled a new quarter-staff from behind his back. Eagerly I traced its lines, then frowned. I couldn't place the material.

'What is it made of?'

'It's titanium. A metal stronger than steel and only slightly less heavy than iron.' It took a few seconds for this information to sink in, but when it did, my smile hurt my cheeks.

'This is why you've had me training with the iron staff.' He nodded, and I ran my fingers along the shaft.

'The weight of the iron we trained with should have given you a significant advantage when using a lighter weapon.' I threw my arms around him and kissed him soundly, ignoring the fact we could be interrupted at any moment. He briefly returned the embrace, staring at me with a hot look that melted me to my core, but then gently pushed me aside. 'You have this session to get used to the weight and balance. I hope you won't need it but...' I understood. Raz was an unparalleled warrior. I turned to

the practice dummies and prepared for a long morning.
Everything depended on this.

'RISE AND SHINE, ladies. Today is your lucky day." I
rolled my eyes. We made our own luck. Looking down at
the garments that had been set aside for me, I grinned
gleefully. No stupid dresses, just a fitted chain mail shirt in
the same material as my bracers and a soft leather jerkin to
go underneath to prevent chafing. There were also leather
pants that moulded to my curves like a glove, allowing for
easy movement as I tested their flexibility with satisfaction.
I tied my flaxen hair loosely at my neck then waited at the
door for the field to go down. With a brief hiss the door
opened and I stepped out.

The other three Breeders scheduled to be Chosen
today also exited, Armana flashing me a hesitant smile as I
walked past. She was dressed in a flowing white robe that
somehow made her seem mysterious, yet that smile made
my stomach clench. Armana was a seer, and I wondered
what she had seen when she looked to our future. We were
led to a waiting room just outside the Arena, which had
been opened for the day into a large stadium, big enough
to fit hundreds of thousands. Armana beckoned me over.
'Come here Asha. I will braid your hair for you.' Not an
offer to refuse if I ended up fighting. I settled myself
between her legs as she began her work. When our guards
exited, she leaned in close and whispered to me, 'You will
have to fight for your dreams today, Asha.' She tugged at
my hair and the slight pain pulled me out of my momen-
tary panic. 'I have a favour to ask.'

'What is it?' I murmured, careful to keep my lips as still
as possible, in case they had a lip reader.

She buried her face in my hair before she answered, effectively hiding her request. 'Make sure he can't take any of us.' I twisted around and the fear in her eyes was my undoing.

'I promise.' She nodded and the other two, who had been watching the exchange, breathed a sigh of relief.

Our security returned and led us upstairs, to where our first partners were seated. Rowan smiled nervously at me as I sat beside him, but his eyes flicked immediately back to the arena where ten men were already battling for four women's favour. Only the strongest four would become part of a breeding triad, their choice in order of their rank, a knockout equalling elimination. It was brutal. Both Edan and Raz appeared to be the best fighters, and were attempting to pick off the weakest. Despite my warrior status, my stomach churned at the brutality. Finally, there were only three left: Edan, Raz and Cade. I saw Cade's eyes dart between Raz and Edan before he made a choice and swung his staff scythe-like at my love. Edan blocked easily but Raz had used Cade's attack to press his advantage and at that moment, clubbed Edan over the back of the head. Edan crumpled. Raz continued his assault and soon Cade was on the floor as well.

Raz turned to grin triumphantly at me, then faced the Council's box. 'I claim Asha Korbani as my partner in accordance with the laws of Choosing.'

Rowan whispered urgently, 'Are you sure you want to do this?' I nodded, glaring at Raz as I stood up, facing the Council.

'I claim the right of Challenge.' Murmurs rode through the crowd. A Challenge had never taken place, not in the years since the nuclear fallout, since we discovered our infertility. Most accepted the Darwinian concept, survival of the fittest, but not I. No way would I become Raz's little brood mare punching bag.

The Council debated amongst themselves, then the elder stepped forward. 'So be it, Asha Korbani. Select your weapon and enter the Arena.' Rowan took my hand and led me to the anteroom where Edan had hidden my quarterstaff. I kissed him gently before I stepped into the Arena.

Raz smirked.

'Just because I've finished a battle Asha, doesn't mean I am tired. In fact,' he adjusted himself in his pants and I saw that the fighting, or perhaps the prospect of drawing my blood, had turned him on. 'I'm more than happy with this turn of events.'

I didn't bother replying, just settled myself into defensive stance and waited. I didn't have to wait long. Raz feinted right then swung aggressively at my ribs. Blocking it was more difficult than I had expected, so I tracked quickly left, resolving to be smarter, use Raz's strength against him. The attack came from the left again and instead of blocking, I used the momentum of his swing to twirl around him, my titanium quarterstaff slamming into his spine, knocking the bastard to the ground.

Fury burned in his eyes as he glared up at me. 'Been holding back in our sessions have you, bitch? That's the last shot you'll get at me.' He came at me with staff spinning in a blur, almost too fast for me to block. Before I knew it, I had been backed into the Arena wall.

'Move Asha!! Move!' Armana's screech distracted me for a split second, enough that I failed to block Raz's next strike properly and fell to my hands and knees, pain exploding through my head, radiating from the blow to my cheek. He chuckled, grabbed hold of my braid and jerked my head backwards. My hands flailed desperately in the sand.

'Yield, Asha.' He leaned in closer, licking the blood from the wound he had opened on my cheek. 'Yield and I won't hurt you too badly our first time.' His sinister smile filled me with determination. 'Though I can't promise anything afterwards.' Then my fingers touched my lifeline.

I struck backwards with the butt of the staff, crushing his kneecap and sending him crumpling to the ground. Staggering to my feet I fought a wave of dizziness to spit down on him. 'No more talking, mother fucker.' I smashed the staff into his jaw, once, twice and a third time for luck. Then, before the Council guards could reach me, I ground his manhood into the sand with the titanium tip, mangling it irreparably. 'Good luck healing that,' I smiled through his screams. 'You'll never get the chance to touch another Breeder.'

As the guards led me towards the Council box, I shot a look at Armana and nodded. Her grin was worth any possible punishment. It lit up the stars.

I stood defiantly before the Council, ready to receive judgement. Or reward. I wasn't sure which yet as I had possibly destroyed their best warrior. The elder came forward.

'By right of Challenge you may choose the second partner for your triad, Asha Korbani. Though I would suggest,' he sighed. 'That you and your partners leave the capital and settle elsewhere.' His eyes followed a screaming, raging Raz. 'Preferably an undisclosed location.'

I grinned. 'I choose warrior Edan Clearwater to join in this triad with his brother, Rowan Clearwater.' The elder nodded.

'So be it. Go and claim your partners.'

I held my head high as I strode from the Arena, blood pouring from my split cheek. The roar of the crowd was deafening, but I only had eyes for the two men who stood at the Arena entrance. Rowan hauled me into his arms, kissing me tenderly as he sent healing energy through my body. By the time he was finished I felt fantastic, skin tingling with the remnants of his light. Edan had moved in behind me, obviously healed by others as I battled. He pressed into my back, sandwiching me between him and his brother and my breath caught as need raced through me. 'Shall we head back to our room and celebrate?' He didn't wait for an answer, throwing me over his shoulder and racing through the corridors to my room. It would remain ours for one night before we would leave to start our new adventure. Rowan raced behind us, snatching the electromagnetic key he had been given to my room and chains from around his neck. He swiped open the door and Edan threw me onto the bed.

'Well, are you going to remove these now?' I gave my wrists a little shake in their direction. Rowan swiped the card across both cuffs, deactivating them, then both of my partners released a wrist each. Pale skin formed a stripe across my tanned arms, but that small imperfection meant one thing to me: freedom.

'Now,' Edan said as he pushed me backwards. 'It's time to claim our prize.'

I laughed, then devoured them with my eyes as both started removing their clothing. All of Rowan's slim, golden flesh, too toned for the healer stereotype, begged to be touched. Yet right next to him was Edan's muscular physique, the ultimate warrior, just a shade darker than his brother. How could anyone choose one? 'I think I am the one who has won the prize.' Rowan crawled up my chest, taking my mouth in a bruising kiss, turning me into molten lava. I reached upwards, running my hands through his thick black hair as Edan began to trail kisses up my inner thighs. My breath caught as Rowan's mouth moved to my breasts, tracing a spiral around my nipple. He sucked it into his mouth, flicking it rhythmically with his tongue. I moaned, the sensations sheer bliss.

Just then Edan's tongue found my sweet spot, alternating light flicks with firmer spirals. My hips ground into his face, urging him on to greater heights. Rowan crawled further up the bed, knees on either side of my face as his cock waved tantalisingly above me. 'I dream of your lips around me, Ash. Every god-damn night I dream it.' Eagerly, I swirled my tongue around the head while I stroked the shaft, delighted when I heard him groan and start thrusting into me. I couldn't take all of it at this angle, so I sucked in my cheeks to create some more pressure. 'God yes, baby, just like that.' Edan took that moment to remind me of his presence, slipping a finger into my tight sheath while still swirling that talented tongue around my clit.

'So tight,' he said, right before he added a second, then a third finger curling them upwards so they hit that spot inside me that was bound to make me blow. I groaned onto Rowan's shaft and immediately he pulled out.

'As good as that was, that's not where I want to finish.' His lips returned to my breasts as Edan crawled up my chest to steal a heated kiss. I squirmed as his tip rubbed back and forth against my clit. Edan pulled my arse to the edge of the bed while Rowan nestled behind me pinching my nipple gently and stroking my clit with his other hand. Lining himself up with my heat, Edan thrust forward to the hilt. I screamed in ecstasy, the mild pinching pain nothing compared to the feeling of having him inside me. Rowan pulled my head back for a kiss as Edan began to languidly stroke inside me, bringing me to a fever pitch. 'Come for us now, Ash.' Rowan's whispered words hit a switch inside me and I screamed my orgasm as Edan emptied his seed inside me in three furious pumps, holding himself still as I rode through the aftershocks. Eventually he pulled out, only to switch places with Rowan.

I looked up at my other lover, licking my lips. Rowan smiled. 'Like what you see?'

I smiled, the cat who got the cream. 'I suppose it's all right.'

He let out an incredulous laugh. 'I want you to ride me,' he demanded, laying down and stoking his long, thick cock as we changed positions. I trailed my hands down his chest as I rubbed my slickness against him, leaning in for a kiss. Agonisingly slowly I lowered myself onto him. I threw my head back, revelling in the sensations as I rocked back and forth on him, grinding my clit with each movement. It wasn't long before I felt like I was on the verge again, but Rowan grasped my hips, holding me still. Edan gently pushed me forwards.

'Now to make us a true triad.' I tensed a little, not sure if I could accommodate both of them at once, despite my arse having been used by them before for our entertainment. The Council only seemed to care about what would make babies, anything else was within limits. 'Relax, Asha. You know you can do this. Think of how good it will feel.' Edan's reassurance relaxed me immediately. A cool liquid slid onto my pucker, and Edan spread it around, then inside my anus, while the other hand coated his cock. Thank god it was Edan and not Rowan, though no doubt they had planned this beforehand.

First one, then two fingers breached my rear, scissored, then thrust a few times until I was moaning again and grinding on Rowan's cock. The fingers were removed then the blunt head of Edan's cock pushed into me. Tears blurred my eyes at the delicious burn, and I wasn't sure I would be able to take much more as he worked it into me, but finally Edan's balls rested on my arse cheeks. We lay like that for a while as I adjusted, Rowan snaking his hand down to rub circles on my clit. Soon I was desperate, and my men began a gentle seesaw movement that had me moaning in ecstasy. The tempo increased—as did the force of their thrusts—when, finally, I screamed my orgasm, my men bellowing as they made their final thrusts and emptied themselves into me. Edan gently slid out then Rowan rolled me to the side, still inside me. I raised a lazy eyebrow, earning a cheeky grin.

'I don't want to leave my new favourite place just yet.'

I laughed, exhausted yet replete. Two hands stroked my back as I started to drift off, a smile on my face.

'Asha?' Edan's voice floated through my sleep-fogged brain.

'Mmm.'

'What do you think about going to the country? Finding a place of our own?'

I rolled over, his suggestion filling me with joy. 'I think,' I said, kissing first Edan then his brother. 'I think that sounds wonderful, as long as we are together.'

Rowan drew me towards him and I snuggled into his chest, Edan spooning around my back, semi hard cock nestled between my butt cheeks. I smiled, drifting into a long sleep. There was nowhere I'd rather be.

Cold, Gold Chains

BY SHANNON SLIQUE

ALL EYES FOLLOWED THE MAGNIFICENT, tall redhead as she sashayed across the hotel lobby towards the exclusive bar area. The broad brimmed hat tilted on an angle complemented the black and white ensemble that pinched in at her tiny waist. The six-inch heels would have toppled a lesser woman but for this woman, they added to her presence.

Sam smiled to himself. Others could look, but she belonged to him and he had the contract to prove it.

She eased a tote with an expensive brand label displayed onto the spare chair at the table where he waited and sat down.

He reached out and placed a hand on the back of her neck and urged her towards him. She didn't resist. She always appeared eager. That was in the contract too. He kissed her long and deep, staking his claim.

'Rhianna. It's lovely to see you. Have you been shopping?'

'Oh no, not today.' Her emerald green eyes flashed a

smile at him. 'Instead, I've been gathering up some things to pass on.' She smiled at the waitress who delivered an icy glass of lemon, lime and bitters. Rhianna's tongue peeked out a millisecond before her lips moulded themselves around the straw for her to suck the liquid.

Sam went hard. It didn't matter how often he saw her, how often he watched her, his body reacted the same way —every damn time.

'I've brought a new contract.' He lay his hand on her arm and stroked it. He felt her quiver.

She tilted her head on one side, pouted her lips and let the bottom lip drop just a little. 'Let's deal with the old one first.' She licked a drop of moisture from her top lip and withdrew an affidavit from the tote.

'What's this?'

'Completion of the old contract. This says that both parties have fulfilled their obligations, that no child has resulted, that there will be no further redress sought by either party in relation to the expired contract and that all confidentiality clauses remain binding in perpetuity.'

'Is that necessary?' Sam frowned as he took the affidavit from her.

'This is the clean slate,' she replied. 'We move forward from here.'

'Who drew this up for you? I thought we were keeping the terms of the contract secret. Who is this Ni-am-h Kelly person?'

'Her name is pronounced 'Neev' and she's me in another skin. We go way back.'

'I know the person you mean. She's tall but dresses like she's a sack of potatoes? Blue eyes, short black hair? Big black glasses.'

'That's the one.'

Sam skimmed the document. 'I can sign this, but we need a witness.' He looked around. 'There's Bree Taylor.'

'She's a lawyer?'

Sam nodded as he caught Bree's eye and gestured for her to come over. 'You want her to witness the new contract?'

'Not yet, we'll come to that later.'

'Rhianna…'

'Hi Sam!' A glowing Bree stood beside the table, her gaze twitching between the pair.

'Hey Bree, we wondered if you'd mind witnessing Rhianna and I sign this document? It's a bit of an imposition in a social setting, so feel free to tell us to run a mile.'

'Not at all!' she punctuated each word. 'You want me to read it?'

'Not necessary. We're both okay with the content.'

'All righty. Rhianna, is it? You go first. Good, now Sam. And me. Great. All done. Have a good night, you two.'

'Thanks Bree. I'll put fifty bucks against your tab.'

'That's not necessary, but I'll take it!' She laughed as she wandered off in the direction of her group.

Rhianna stood, gathering up one copy of the affidavit. She leaned down and took Sam's mouth with hers in a spine-melting kiss, ignoring any audience.

'I've got to go. I'll leave this with you.' She handed over the tote.

Sam glanced inside and saw at least a dozen jewellery boxes from the store where he had bought necklaces, bracelets and anklets for Rhianna over the past thirty months.

'I'm confused.'

'Don't be. These are your chains from our time together. I'm returning them to you because, with the contract ended, they don't bind me or you anymore. The keys to the flat are in there too. Goodbye, Sam.'

'Rhianna…' Sam stood in a daze as she walked away.

RHIANNA MOVED AS QUICKLY as she could across the foyer and down the escalator to the hotel forecourt where a line of taxis waited. The crack of her stilettos on the hard tile sounded just like the pieces of her heart as they shattered in her chest.

The ride home was a short one. She'd moved from the opulent apartment that Sam provided for her in Docklands and into a well-appointed but cheaper version in the CBD. It wasn't as quiet as Sam's, but it was close to work. She wasn't broke these days—thanks to that damn contract—and she didn't have a student debt either, but she still needed to watch her cash.

She'd thought long and hard about breaking with Sam. Lists of pros and cons littered her workspace. In the end, it was her need to forge her own career, to build her independence and to never again to live in such a threatening level of destitution that had won the day.

Now the deed was done, she was angry with herself. She'd thrown away all that mind-blowing sex for her pride? Surely there could have been a compromise, but it was complicated these days.

She stormed into her flat and flipped off her shoes so forcefully that they bounced off the opposite wall. She tore off the wig and flung it to the floor. She wouldn't be needing that again. It had served its purpose for the last three years, keeping her anonymous or at least keeping her Rhianna persona in place. The green contact lenses were the next to go. She popped them out and returned them to their case out of habit.

Drained, she threw herself onto her couch and burst into tears. The contract had not allowed for any emotional attachment in what was essentially a service agreement. He paid her a six-figure sum and provided an apartment and she paid in sex—glorious, fulfilling, erotic, orgasmic sex. But she'd fallen in love with the self-serving bastard. Six months in, and she'd known she was doomed. And there'd been two years left to run.

Her head flopped against the back of the chair. She'd burnt her bridges. Now she could just be Niamh, A-grade student and first pick for the prestigious Patterson-Prime law firm. During her internship at PP, her skills had caught the eye of Juliet Prime and as soon as she'd graduated, Niamh had been employed in their business acquisitions area protecting their clients from marauding corporate raiders.

This meant that she was often in the same room as Sam Fredericks as he went about wheeling and dealing and building his empire with little concern for those whose businesses he consumed. It showed her another side to the lover who came to her bed. This Sam was driven, brooked no disagreement and rarely engaged in social niceties.

Niamh had been terrified that he'd recognise her, but he looked at her no more than was necessary to size up any possible weakness in her arguments. He didn't flirt. Rather, he seemed to dismiss the young woman wearing her shapeless dresses, big glasses and subservient attitude, though his eyes returned time and again to the pendant that nestled just above the shadow of her breasts.

With Rhianna gone, Niamh could start coming out of her shell. The formless dresses could morph into business suits and soon Niamh could be as confident and sassy as her alter-ego. Then she'd be ready to take on Sam Fredericks when he finally made the connection between Niamh and Rhianna.

She stood, gathered up the wig and the shoes and slouched towards her bedroom. She dumped the wig in the trash. The dress was hung at the back of the cupboard. The shoes went back into their box and joined the dozen or so similar boxes in the side shelf. If only her memories could be so easily stacked away.

She showered and slipped on her silky cami and g-string and fell into bed. It was early yet, but the past couple of hours left her feeling like she'd run a marathon.

As she reached for the light, she heard what sounded like a knock on her door. The building was still unfamiliar to her, so she couldn't be sure if it was her door or another further along the corridor. She ignored it. The sound came again, firmer this time.

She retrieved her kimono, slid her arms into it and went to check. Leaving the chain in place, she eased the door open to find a furious Sam Fredericks. He held the tote in one hand.

'Ms Kelly. May I come in?'

'I think it's better that you leave, Mr Fredericks. I was in bed.'

'All the better, Ms Kelly. But unless you want me to flatten this fucking door, I think you should open it properly.' His tone was controlled but definite—the same tone she had witnessed in his business negotiations, but never with Rhianna.

Niamh stood back, wrapped the kimono firmly around herself and tightened the belt before unlatching the chain and opening the door wide.

SAM STOOD IRRESOLUTE. He was having second thoughts about the wisdom of his actions. What if he'd guessed wrong? This young woman had a sharp mind that was already highly regarded in legal circles. He'd be a pariah if this little fiasco became known.

She turned away and it cleared the haze that his thoughts had drawn him into.

'Would you like a cup of tea?'

'Coffee.' He hesitated. Rhianna would know that.

'Take a seat. I won't be long.'

'Rhianna…'

Her head whipped towards him.

'Is not here.'

'I think she is.'

'Where? Hiding in the bedroom, perhaps?'

'Let's go and check.' He strode towards the only other open door in the place. He flung open the wardrobe and riffled through the clothes that were hanging there, eventually arriving at the black and white outfit, and pulled it out. He caught sight of the discarded hair and grabbed that up too.

'Now would you like to explain what the fuck is going on and why you've been playing me for a fool?'

Niamh slumped.

'Come out to the kitchen.'

Sam held the dress and wig in one hand as he strode after her.

'Explain.'

'About three years ago, I was half way through my degree without enough money to keep going. I created Rhianna to go and find work that Niamh couldn't. Niamh had to protect her reputation as a law student and couldn't afford any taint to her name. You met Rhianna and she was the person you wanted to fuck, so that's who you got.'

She shrugged one shoulder. 'You wouldn't have wanted goody-two-shoes Niamh, anyhow. For two and a half years, you never asked me what I did with myself during the day, so I got on with my study, and waited for you at night.'

'And you were laughing up your sleeve at me the whole time?'

'No!' She dropped her head and then raised her chin to look at him. 'About six months into our contract, I wanted to tell you, but you made some comment about how good it was that we didn't have to air all our private stuff to each other to be able to have great sex. I figured explaining about Niamh/ Rhianna would have been way too personal, so I locked it away. But I couldn't let it go on any longer. I knew you were thinking about another contract, but that wasn't going to happen. It was much too risky when I was seeing you every other week in my workplace or yours. And I was working longer hours. Rhianna had to go.'

Sam threw down the dress and wig and stepped forward. He took hold of her upper arms and studied her eyes before crashing his mouth to hers. He sucked hard on her top lip and then her tongue until she mewled against his mouth. He pulled his head back to gauge her reaction.

She slid her hands over his chest to flick open the buttons on his shirt. 'This isn't part of the contract.'

'There is no contract, remember? Just you and me, no matter what you call yourself.'

His hand went to the belt of her kimono and pulled it loose. 'Thank God Niamh likes sexy night wear,' he growled as he lifted her onto the kitchen bench. His mouth dropped to one rock hard nipple that poked against the soft fabric. He sucked at it, pink silk and all. He pushed the kimono from her shoulders. One hand slithered down to cup her mound and edge aside the scrap of cloth he found there.

Her hands speared into his hair as she leaned back to grant him full access to her body. Her legs wrapped around his thighs and hugged him to her. She could feel his rock-hard shaft between her legs.

Her body flexed against his hand, driving his searching fingers further inside. His thumbnail flicked her clit and sent her hurtling into oblivion.

He pulled back and laughed, hearty and relieved. 'It's you! It really is you. Thank God. I thought I'd lost you.' He pulled her into a fireman's lift and started walking.

'This isn't a very romantic position for me.'

Sam breathed deeply of her intimate fragrance. 'It is for me.' He inhaled again before sitting her on the bed, whisking off her teddy and lowering her back against the sheets. He went down on his knees between her legs and rested his face on her stomach, breathing slowly as her hand brushed against his hair. 'I went to the flat but there was nothing left of you there. Not even a toothbrush. You were gone.'

'What made you come here?'

His hands whispered over her breasts and his thumbs barely hovered over her nipples in the way he knew she loved. 'Initially it was because Rhianna and Niamh were connected. I called in a favour to get your home address from the company database.'

He felt her fingers stiffen on his head. 'That's unethical, Mr Fredericks.'

'I didn't give a fuck about that. I was desperate.' His thumbs and forefingers massaged the raspberry nubs. 'Then I thought about you saying that Niamh was "me in another skin". Something clicked.' His tongue dipped into her belly button and he felt her gasp. His hands trailed down over her abdomen and homed together to arrive at her thighs and draw them apart.

'What I felt with Rhianna, I hadn't felt for anyone before. But on those days when you were sitting in meetings with me, I felt compelled to do with Niamh what I did with Rhianna.' He licked the skin of her belly. 'You have this presence, an essence maybe, that I can't ignore. I thought I was hallucinating.'

His tongue trailed a path down to her mound. 'You'll remember that the nights after those meetings, we always fucked harder and faster. And then we did it all over again because I wanted Rhianna and I wanted Niamh.'

'And we both wanted you.' His mouth found her clit. 'Ah… I thought it was because you got frustrated that my arguments were more persuasive than what your team offered, and you had to let off steam.'

'Oh, that added a little piquancy.' Lick. Nibble. 'I wanted to know what was hiding under those potato sacks.'

His hands stretched up so that his fingers could again grasp her beaded nipples and rotate them ever so slightly.

'They are very elegant, very expensive, potato sacks designed specifically to keep minds like yours off my body.'

He smiled against her mound. 'It didn't work. Not for me at least. Now you must pay for every millisecond of agony you put me through—then and now.' He dragged his fingernails from her breasts to her hips.

'No fair,' she gasped. 'You have trained my body to react instantly.'

'I know. Your juices will be wetting that scrap between your legs. I'll take care of that.' He moved away to pull the fabric down her legs. He was back in a moment, spreading her legs wide and lapping up the wetness that flowed from her.

'Sam. Stop!' He pulled back instantly. 'Get undressed. I couldn't bear you to stop later...'

He placed his hands on the bed on either side of her body and levered himself off the floor. Niamh sat up and worked on his belt while he shrugged out of his shirt.

'Do you want a condom?' he asked.

'We haven't used one for years. Why now?' Those startling blue eyes narrowed at him.

'No contract. Just checking.'

'We're good, unless you've been tom-catting in the last three hours?'

He chuckled as she slid the zip down and took hold of his shaft through his jocks.

'There's only one woman I want and she's right here, teasing my balls off.'

Niamh kept kneading his rod as he toed off his shoes. He stepped back and shrugged out of the rest of his clothes to stand naked in front of her.

She grasped his hips and pulled him forward inhaling deeply. 'I love the scent of your musk,' she muttered as her mouth claimed his cock, licking its length as one hand massaged the tight sacs at its base. Her tongue swirled around the top like his shaft was a dripping popsicle just squeezed from its sheath. She took it deep into her throat.

He bucked. Her hands grasped his butt cheeks to keep him positioned where she wanted him. 'I can't...' he started before pulling himself out of her mouth, pushing her back and spearing his full length hard into her body.

She screamed as she went into instant orgasmic overload, her muscles pulsing along his length. Sam pumped, his balls slapping against her, until he reached his own straining peak releasing his essence with a guttural cry.

His body held taut for almost a minute until he slowly came back to earth and collapsed on the bed beside her.

'Darling…'

'No endearments.'

'No contract.'

'Why the contract anyway?'

'Greed, lust, desire. I wanted all of you all to myself and I wanted you to know it. Why thirty months?'

'Initially to test whether you were serious about it and then to see me through my degree. And the chains? Those cold, gold chains?'

He lifted himself to look down at her and took her face in his hands. 'Didn't you work it out? If I chained you to the bed by your neck to fuck you however I wanted, I bought you a necklace. If I manacled your feet or your wrists, I found an anklet or a bracelet. It was my way of saying thank you for going along with my erotic fantasies.'

'They were my fantasies too. I loved you taking total control of my body. You showed me things I would never have known were possible. And when it was reversed, well, need I say more?' She double-flicked her eyebrows at him.

'Minx.' He nipped her earlobe. 'The jewellery was to show that I cared about you beyond the damn contract. That you meant something to me. You should know that I chose every last chain with care. They were reminders that you and I, we're totally bound, whether there's a contract in place or not.'

'Not ownership? You weren't planning on linking them all together to lock me up and throw away the key?'

'I should have thought of that, but no.' He shook his head wryly. 'Why did you give them back?'

'That part of my life is over.'

'I noticed you kept one.'

'Just one. It was special. Chosen with care.'

'I thought I noticed Niamh wearing it in the meetings. It was never on full display, but the glimpses I got made me curious. A diamond-studded crucifix surrounded by a golden heart looked sweet on Niamh but seductive as all hell on Rhianna. I was going to have sharp word with the jeweller. She said it was a one-off.'

He smiled as his hands travelled over her ears. 'I like your hair. It's nicer than the wig.'

'You knew it was a wig?'

'Day dot.'

'You didn't say…'

'Too personal—contract, remember?'

'And the eyes?'

'Didn't pick that. I love both the blue and the green. So… how about a new contract? Of the marital variety?'

He felt her stiffen. 'But you don't want to be married, wife, kids, picket fence…'

'Picket fence might be a bit much, but the rest, yeah—with the right woman. That's what I was going to offer Rhianna tonight. She left me standing. I'm asking Niamh instead. Be mine forever?'

'Is Niamh the consolation prize?'

Sam jerked back and studied her face.

'No!' He struggled to find the words to explain. 'I can't separate the two of you. It's like a part of me always knew you were one and the same.'

'It'll be problematic sitting on opposite sides of a meeting table.'

'You've been running rings around my team, I might have to look for a new acquisitions firm. Any suggestions?'

'I'll think about it while I do this.' She reached down to tease his shaft back into wakefulness.

'And the contract?' Two fingers scissored into her body. Two could play this game.

'You'll have to convince me.' She dipped her head to suckle one of his nipples.

'Woman, you'll be the death of me. An excruciatingly slow, exhausting, erotic kind of death.'

Niamh straddled him and looked down into his deep, violet eyes. 'That's my plan. Every day and every night for the rest of our lives. It's a long road. We'd best get started.' She lowered her face towards his.

Chains of Love

BY SONIA CAINE

BETHANY STOOD IN HER BEDROOM, staring at her reflection in the full-length mirror, and gasped in horror. 'I can't leave the house looking like this.'

'You can and you will, Beth.' Her best friend Sally got off the bed, stood next to her and smiled. 'You look fantastic. If Caleb could see you now he'd be so sorry he dumped you for that skanky Georgette.'

'I'm dressed exactly like skanky Georgette, so does that make me one too? And why do I have to dress like this to go to that new club you've been talking about?'

'You are nothing like Georgette, class radiates from you no matter how you're dressed. And you have to dress like that because they won't let you in wearing your church mouse ensemble. God, why would anyone who had a body like yours hide beneath those long denim skirts and floral shirts you like so much?' Sally shook her head and flopped back down on the bed.

Taking a deep breath, Bethany ran her hands down her hips. The skirt—if she could call it that—was made out of some garbage bag material that clung to her and sat just beneath her butt cheeks. The blood red, skin-tight top with a plunging V neckline exposed most of her breasts and sat precariously close to her nipples. If she moved too much, she was sure she'd experience a nip slip. Dancing was out of the question.

Then there was the makeup. Sally had applied it with a heavy hand and now Bethany was unrecognisable. Her red lips matched her top and black eyeshadow seemed to make her blue eyes glow. Her long honey brown hair hung in lose waves past her shoulders. This was not what a minister's daughter looked like. Her dad would have a fit if he could see her now.

But as she looked at her reflection, at the woman she hardly recognised, a buzz of excitement sizzled through her body and she smiled. For one night she would love to not have to worry about the restrictions of her upbringing; she wanted to forget about Caleb and experience something a little different.

'Your body is freaking hot,' Sally said as if she knew Bethany was admiring herself, and tugged her hand, pulling her towards the door. 'Let's go so we can show it off.'

THE PULSING of heavy metal music vibrated from every part of the club and pounded up from the floor and through Bethany's feet. The dark room, lit only by tiny pinprick lights in the ceiling and neon writing on the walls, was filled with people dancing to the noise—she couldn't call what she was hearing music.

A metal sign hung from the ceiling read, Chains and His Church of Sinners. It was unlike any 'church' Bethany had ever known.

They moved further into the room and Bethany bumped into someone. 'Oh sorry,' she said and saw that the guy she'd hit had a girl pressed up against the wall, her legs wrapped firmly around his waist. He turned his head, gave Bethany a once over and smiled suggestively. 'Hey baby, wanna join in?' The woman he was pressing into buried her face in his neck then reached out to slide a hand down Bethany's arm.

'Umm, I'll pass. Thanks,' she said and stumbled back. The guy shrugged and began pounding into the woman.

'Where the hell have you taken me?' Bethany shouted into Sally's ear.

'Isn't it fantastic?' Sally's smile was almost as bright as the neon writing.

'That guy's having sex up against a wall!' Bethany pointed over her shoulder. This wasn't what she meant by experiencing something different.

Sally glanced in the direction Bethany pointed. 'I only see a girl giving some guy head.'

The temptation to turn and look was surprisingly strong, but she held firm. The more she scanned the club, the more of the same was going on in every dark corner or right in the middle of the dance floor. Desire curled in her stomach at the sight—a feeling she was unaccustomed to—and she shivered. She liked dinner and coffee with friends and if she felt a bit rowdier, there was a jazz bar she liked to go to and have a glass of Moscato while she listened to the sexy sounds of the saxophone. This was not a place for her. 'Sally, I should go.'

'No, Beth, you can't. You need a bit of fun and excitement. You've been living like a nun for too long. You're twenty-three and you dress and act like my fifty-year-old mother.'

Bethany sucked in a sharp breath and for a beat, guilt

crossed Sally's face. 'Beth, I'm sorry. I didn't mean that. But you could loosen up a little.'

Was Sally right? Did she live like a fifty-year-old nun? She nibbled her bottom lip and looked around the room. One night couldn't hurt could it? Her glance flicked back to the guy she'd bumped into. The woman had him pressed up against the wall and was on her knees in front of him. With his eyes open into slits, he smiled and nodded his head for her to go to him. Bethany took a step forward then shook herself. This place was not only sinful but dangerous. And her blood pounded with excitement.

'I'll stay for an hour,' she told Sally.

Sally clapped her hands and jumped up and down. Her breasts threatening to spill from the flimsy top she wore. 'I'm going to the bar to get us a drink and then we'll dance.'

Bethany didn't want to be left alone, but Sally took off before she could follow and she was left standing amongst a bunch of overly stimulated bodies.

While waiting for Sally, a guy asked her to join him in the 'party room' for strip poker, and another guy asked her to go with him to the 'show room' to take part in an orgy. Her heart thumped in time with the music at their suggestions, but she refused. When she told Sally she needed a bit of excitement in her life, she hadn't expected this. She didn't know whether to strangle Sally for bringing her here, or thank her for showing her there's more to life than quiet dinners with friends. This was excitement on steroids, but was she ready for it?

As she searched for her friend through the crowd, Bethany spotted a man watching her from across the room. It was dark, but even from a distance she could feel his gaze as if he was physically touching her. Her mouth watered, breath quickened, and she couldn't look away.

This stranger in the crowd had her complete attention and a strong force propelled her to go to him.

Then Sally came rushing towards her, without their drinks, breaking the connection. Bethany moved her head from side to side to peer over Sally's shoulders, but the man had disappeared. Frowning, she scanned the room but there were too many people for her to see where he went.

'This hot guy at the bar wants to take me into the party room. Is it bad if I go? I told him I needed to check with you first, but I'll stay if you want me too.'

Bethany had her own hot guy she wanted to find. Even though it was dark, and she couldn't see him clearly, she knew that man was scorching. The way he looked at her was indication enough.

'Go have fun. I'll be fine.'

'Are you sure?'

Bethany nodded.

Sally smiled. 'Go and have fun too.' She gave Bethany a quick hug before she turned and ran back towards the bar.

Whoever thought her best friend was such a wild thing? Sometimes you never really completely know a person. She laughed and shook her head. Tonight, she didn't really know herself either. If someone said she'd be in a place like this and finding it thrilling she would have scoffed in their face. But something inside her wanted to break out from the restrictions of her very moral, church attending upbringing. It couldn't hurt to explore new things, if only for a night.

And she knew exactly who she wanted to explore, she just needed to find him. Walking towards the place she last saw him, she needed to push her way through the crowded dance floor. As she reached the other side, she stumbled and an arm caught her around the waist before she face-planted the floor. Her back pressed up against a solid chest and the arm around her waist was strong and firm. Warm breath, sweet with liquor fanned over her neck. 'Easy, honey.'

The deep voice sent a wave of desire down her spine and pooled into her belly. Without seeing who was behind her, she knew it was the man she'd seen earlier. There was a pull she'd felt before that had her tied to him now. Bethany turned her head and caught sight of his full lips, tilted in a crooked smile. Her gaze travelled along a square jaw line and up to the greenest eyes she'd ever seen, surrounded by thick dark lashes. A lock of black hair hung over his forehead. The desire that was dancing around her belly now darted between her legs. Her body reacted to him like it had never done before and with a will of its own. She pressed up against him.

He sucked in a breath and turned her to face him. Bethany's breath stopped all together. He stood a head taller than her, even in her deathly high heels, and his black hair flicked out at the collar of his white shirt. Even under the fabric she could see a firm and muscled body. He looked like a beautiful devil.

He kept his hands on the curve of her hips. His heated gaze had her burning from the inside out. 'You're new here. Wanting to join in on the fun, but haven't built up the courage yet.'

How long had he been watching her? It should have concerned her, but it didn't. This whole situation should be alarming but, somehow, she wanted it. She hadn't been truly ready to participate, but with him she was one hundred percent in attendance.

'Why haven't you indulged in some fun?' The hands on her hips made stroking motions and her legs turned into cooked spaghetti.

'Umm… I…' Her words stuck in her throat.

He trailed a finger from her collar bone down the length of the plunging V of her top and back up. Her nipples hardened and peaked through the thin fabric. His gaze dropped to her chest and his tongue darted out and licked his bottom lip. She inwardly groaned, but then his eyes pierced hers and he grinned. Maybe she'd groaned out loud. God, what was happening to her?

'I can see you've been tempted. Perhaps you're shy? Although, I'm very happy you haven't tried anything yet.'

'You are? Why?' She finally found her voice, though it was shaky and breathless. Even as they stood on the edge of a dance floor—music pounding at ear damaging levels—it felt like they were the only two people in the room.

'Why?' He flashed her white straight teeth when he smiled. 'Because I get you all to myself.'

'Oh…' Was all she could manage to say, words leaving her again.

'Come with me,' he said as he took her hand and led her past the bar and up a set of stairs. She probably shouldn't be going anywhere with him. She didn't know him. But wasn't this club all about letting go? And with the way he looked at her—and how her body responded to him—she'd follow him anywhere. It was lust at first sight. She needed to get her hands on his body.

At the top of the stairs a man stood in front of a timber door. 'Hey Todd, you can take off.'

'No worries, Chains,' the guy replied.

Chains… his name is Chains? She remembered the sign downstairs: Chains and His Church of Sinners. He must be the owner of this club. 'You need a hand with your lady? I'd be happy to offer my services,' Todd said as his gaze lingered over Bethany's chest.

'Nah, mate. I can manage.'

'Maybe I can help you with the next one.' Todd grinned, then jogged down the stairs.

When they entered the room, Bethany was surprised to find it was the complete opposite to the club. Downstairs was dark and moody and this room was bright white. The walls, the floor, even the massive bed in the centre of the room, were white. Bethany couldn't keep her eyes off it all. She didn't know this man, but she knew without a doubt she wanted him on that bed.

He moved in behind her and placed his hands on her shoulders, kissing the curve of her neck and setting her body on fire.

'What's your name?' he murmured as the kiss travelled up her neck. She tilted her head back to give him better access and he nibbled at the sensitive spot below her ear. Right where her pulse beat like a drum. Her name? God, she could barely think with his mouth on her skin. 'It's… it's Bethany. But people call me Beth.'

The hands slid down her arms and splayed across her stomach pulling her back against him. His impressive hard-on pushed against her arse and made her wet in an instant.

'I like Bethany. It's sexy… You're fucking sexy.' His hands moved to cup her breasts, massaging in slow torturous circles. 'I noticed you the second you walked into the club and I knew I had to fuck you. But I have a feeling that once I do, I'm not going to want to stop.' The top she wore was now spread open so her breasts were completely exposed and his warm hands on her skin felt like magic. 'And I know that when you saw me, you wanted to fuck me too. But there's something sweet and pure about you. Are you going to be able to handle it?'

'Yes.' With him… absolutely. And to prove it, she led one of his hands down to her thighs, and slid his fingers under her panties. He trembled against her back as he slid a finger in and out of her wet folds. He walked her to the bed and she fell on her stomach onto the soft mattress. Pushing her skirt to her waist, he palmed her arse. 'I want you so fucking bad.' She buried her face in the mattress to muffle her groan. Then he flipped her onto her back, pulled down her panties and spread her thighs apart. 'God, you're beautiful.'

The hungry way he stared at her made her believe she really was. And she didn't want to cover up. Instead, she made quick work of removing her clothes. What was it about this man that had her throwing away all her insecurities? When she was with Caleb, they'd make love with the lights off and under the sheets. She'd never felt comfortable exposing herself so fully.

She couldn't call what she was about to do with Chains making love, but there was nothing she wanted to keep from him. He could take her body, her mind, her soul. All of it. This man was going to do more than bury himself in her body. If she wasn't careful, he'd bury himself into her heart.

'Are you going to keep staring at me or are you going to touch me?' Her voice came out as a husky whisper.

He chuckled low and deep. 'Impatient, are we?'

She bit her lip and nodded.

He knelt on the bed and hovered above her, a hairs breadth away from her lips. She placed a hand on his chest to stop him and he arched a questioning eyebrow. 'I want to see you,' she explained.

Nodding, he stood and went to unbutton his shirt. She shook her head, got onto her knees and removed his hands. 'Let me.'

'Bossy too. My kind of woman.' Though his mouth twitched with laughter, his eyes smouldered with liquid heat.

Her hands trembled with each button and her breaths were raspy—like she'd just finished a race. When the last button gave way, she sighed with relief and spread her hands over his shoulders, pushing the shirt so it dropped to the floor. She gasped. He was built. Rock hard abs, strong ropey arms and tanned skin. But what had her mesmerised was his tattoos. Dozens of intricate chains starting from his chest wove and draped off more tattoos of roses, clocks and skulls. His arms were covered in chains too and when he moved them it looked as if the chains were swaying with the movement. Her fingertips trailed over them and his skin broke out in goosebumps. A set of chains got her attention because they ran under the waistband of his faded jeans, and she definitely wanted to follow. His muscles bunched when she flicked open the fly of his jeans and pulled them down his legs. The chains wrapped around a thick firm thigh, ending with a rose clamped inside a lock. He was a work of art.

Next, the boxer briefs were pushed down and his thick erection sprang free. She wasted no time. She cupped his balls and wrapped her fingers around his cock. He groaned long and low and threw his head back. Not only did she want to touch him—she wanted to taste him. Bethany pressed her lips against the tip and licked the moisture beaded there. Then she took him into her mouth.

'Fuck…' he moaned through clenched teeth and buried his fingers in her hair. She'd never given head before, but the sounds Chains was making made her think she was doing something right. Then, all too quickly, he pulled away. 'I want to be buried in your pussy when I come.'

A shiver ran up her spine as he stepped out of his jeans and joined her on the bed. Anchoring her hands above her head, he pressed into her. But, for once, she wanted to be the one in control. She'd always let Caleb take the lead—now it was her turn.

Bethany pulled her wrists free and pushed Chains onto his back, straddling him and slamming her lips onto his mouth. Rubbing her breasts against his chest, his strong hands grabbed hold her of hips and rocked her against him. As much as she wanted to take her time exploring his magnificent body, she wanted him insider her. She couldn't wait any longer. She was probably going to go to hell for behaving like this. How would she ever walk inside her father's church again? Her father's church, Caleb—all those paths had been ripped up and redirected her to Chains and the Church of Sinners. And she loved it here. Loved having a man who was literally wrapped in chains, snug between her thighs.

Spotting condoms on the bedside table, she grabbed one, opened the foil packet and slowly slid it onto Chains' impressive hard-on. Then, lifting slightly off his lap, she positioned herself so he could slide his cock inside her. She shuddered when he entered.

'You're so wet… so tight.' The words were murmured on a groan. 'You're never leaving this fucking room.'

'Fine with me.' She gasped as he filled and stretched her. Grasping his head, she pulled him up to her breasts wanting them in his mouth. It was exhilarating having so much control and Chains appeared more than happy to hand over the reins.

Their bodies, slick with sweat, stuck together as she rocked against him. She shifted and he slid a hand between them and flicked her clit with his fingers.

Gripping her legs tighter around him, lights, fireworks, explosions went off in her brain and an orgasm that was building exploded and tore through her body. 'Chains…' she cried as she bucked against him.

Chains pounded so hard, her knees bounced off the bed and she held tight to him. His head fell back on a long moan as he found his release and she collapsed on his chest.

When their heavy breathing subsided, Chains rolled Bethany onto her back and propped his head on his hand. He was beautiful, dark and dangerous. Everything she would normally stay away from. Everything her father preached was bad for her. But nothing about him felt bad. In fact, she'd never felt so good—and not because of what he could do with her body. Her heart gave a funny shudder. This man was a stranger, she should be horrified by what she'd just done and making a quick exit. But the way he stared at her with hooded eyes, heat pouring from them, she didn't want to move. In her heart he wasn't a stranger; she couldn't explain it, but he was a part of her.

He trailed a finger over her breast and all coherent thoughts flittered out of her mind as he circled the nipple. Bending his head, he licked it with his warm tongue and her back arched off the mattress. How could she want him again so soon? Then he moved off the bed and Bethany groaned her displeasure.

'You're insatiable,' he said grinning. 'I love it. But you need to know what you're getting yourself into before we continue.' He walked in all his naked glory to a wall Bethany now noticed was covered in flat screen TVs.

With his back towards her—and his back was almost as good as the front—he picked up a control and pointed it to the screens. One by one, they flicked on.

He turned back to her and all the chains tattooed on his body moved and rippled over his skin. Noticing she was distracted, he pointed to the TVs. 'This is my life. The club is mine.' When she'd learned his name was Chains, she'd put two and two together.

Each screen behind him had something different show-ing. 'This room is the show room—our main attraction. Anything and everything goes on in here. The room is made out of glass, so spectators can watch the perfor-mance inside—even participate. This one's the games room. Speaks for itself.' And it did; there where tables of different games set up with people in different stages of undress, some performing sexual acts. 'And we also have a party room.' It was a room with a huge hot tub filled with naked people under a disco ball and laser lights flashing against the walls.

'Why are you showing me this?'

'Because I want you. From the moment I saw you, I knew you were mine.' Bethany's heart fluttered at his words. She'd felt the same way about him. 'But you need to know how I live my life. The things I enjoy and participate in. This isn't your world. I can tell you're different, but you let go tonight and I fucking loved it. But who are you really?'

'I'm a minister's daughter, whose best friend thinks I'm living like a fifty-year-old nun.' Better to lay it all out now. No use in pretending.

'You surely don't act like one.' He smirked.

Heat rushed to her face. She'd acted like a completely different person and she liked the way it made her feel, liked the way Chains made her feel. She couldn't image it could be this good with anyone else, nor would she want to try.

'Can a member of the church of God join the church of sinners?' His gaze held hers. Did she see hope in his eyes?

She got off the bed, not bothering to cover up—for the first time, she felt comfortable in her skin—and stood next to Chains. Watching the TV screens, she saw things she could never have imagined and adrenaline rushed through her veins. From the moment Bethany had walked into the club it had coiled around her, inviting her into its world. Promising her excitement and fantasies. And the longer she stood there watching the TVs, the more she wanted to discard her old life and wrap herself in the one Chains was offering. Except this club showed no signs of anyone caring about monogamy. In the games room, she'd seen one woman move onto three different men. As much as Bethany wanted to be amongst it, she only wanted it with Chains.

Pressing in closer, Chains cupped Bethany's face. 'I understand if you don't want to do this with me. It's not for everyone.' Understanding with a dash of disappointment crossed his face.

'This is all very exciting and I do want this with you but…' She bit her lip, she didn't know how to tell him what she wanted in case she was asking too much.

'But not enough to include this in your life.' He went to step away, but she held onto his hands, stopping him.

'That's not what I was going to say.'

A spark of hope lit his eyes.

Bethany blew out a long breath. If she didn't speak up now, she'd regret it. 'I don't want to share you in there.' Her arm waved towards the screens. 'I don't want another woman touching you, nor do I want any other man but you touching me.'

Chains tipped his head back and laughed and her heart dropped to the floor. Why would she ever think that even for a second, a man like him would want only her too. She turned to collect her clothes so she could leave. She needed to get out of this room before she burst into tears.

'Bethany, stop,' Chains said and grabbed her wrist.

When she turned to face him, his eyes still sparkled

with laughter and anger boiled in her gut making her shake. 'Thanks for a great time. I'll recommend you to all my friends.' She tugged her arm free; she couldn't let him see how hurt she really was. 'As a matter of fact, I think I'll join the party room. Looks like a lot of fun.'

She spun on her heels, but couldn't take a step because two arms wrapped in chains pinned her against his chest. 'Like fuck you will,' he growled in her ear. 'I said you are mine. I'm not a sharing kind of guy.'

The arms holding her tight loosened their grip and slid up her body. His hands cupped her breasts. Her knees shook and her heart hammered. Even though she was hurt and angry with him, desire stronger than any other emotion consumed her. Tilting her head back on his chest she let him run his hands over her body.

'I laughed because I was relieved that you wanted me too. And that you didn't want to share me. Because I sure as hell don't want any other bastard touching you. You are mine and I'm yours. Only yours. There will be no other women. You're the only one I want to fuck.'

It was her turn to laugh, relief at his words washing over her. 'Will we still get to play with each other in those rooms?' she asked, the fifty-year-old nun no longer resided in her body.

'Abso-fucking-lutely!' he growled and spun her around. Picking her up off her feet, he shoved her against the wall and slammed into her. She screamed with pleasure as her legs hooked around his hips and his arms held her securely as he pounded into her. The arms that were covered in chains not only wrapped around her body, but his chains wrapped around her heart.

Melting Snowflakes

BY C M JAMES

'CHAINS REQUIRED BEYOND THIS POINT.'

Liana frowned at the sign. Chains? Whatever for?

The GPS read ten minutes to her destination. She'd get there, get the documents signed and get back on the road to the airport in a half hour, maximum. It was mid-afternoon in late autumn, but it felt darker driving up the mountain with the sun hiding on the other side.

The Board was depending on her. The CFO himself had recommended her. He trusted her. It wasn't because she was the only one with no family, no one at home expecting dinner on the table, no hot date waiting for her to arrive. She blew out the breath she'd been holding. Who was she kidding? She was a glorified courier with a law degree.

It was four degrees Celsius outside, but she was toasty warm with the car heater blowing. The smell of warm hire car leather was comforting. Almost enough to make her forget who she was driving towards.

In and out, apologise for interrupting his holiday, get

the signature and leave. She drummed her fingers on the steering wheel.

She should ask for a raise. The emergency flight out of Sydney with no time to pack anything; the long drive from the airport into the mountains; the freezing weather she was not prepared for. It was the last Friday of the month and she was at the end of her laundry cycle, so she was wearing the slightly see-through blouse, with the too-short skirt and only a light jacket over the top. She was going to freeze the minute she stepped out of the car.

She spotted the sign for the driveway to the property. It wasn't sealed and the sedan that had been a dream on the highway, struggled on the steep, pot-holed surface.

The driveway was lined with tall, peeling eucalyptuses that intensified the shadow cast by the mountainside. She turned a corner and saw the cottage. It was something out of a fairy tale: charming and rustic, built of stone blocks and wooden beams. It looked like it belonged in the English countryside, rather than hitched to the side of an outback Aussie mountain. The garden was barren at this time of year, thorny stems turned grey and brown leaves twisted out of stone-edged flower beds.

She pulled in front of the cottage and shut the engine off. He had better be home. The thickening clouds made her apprehensive. She wished she'd checked the weather before she'd left Sydney. Wrapping the thin coat tightly around her body, Liana grabbed her handbag and the files for signing and braved the cold.

The sharp tang of eucalyptus and the crispness of the air took her breath away. When was the last time she got out of the city? She inhaled deeply, savouring the smell and the silence.

There was no answer at the door. Liana knocked again,

but still nothing. She peered through the window, but it was dark inside. She huffed, breathing warm air into her hands. After travelling all this way, she wasn't about to give up. She pulled her coat tighter, the cold settling into her bare knees. A gravel path led around the side of the house. She followed it around.

There was a strange bubbling sound at the back of the house. Turning the corner, she gasped as she found herself standing directly behind Brett Buchanan, CEO of Buchanan Property, where she'd worked for the last four years. He was stark naked.

She shut her eyes, but not before catching a glimpse of his broad back and tight buttocks. This was not good. She spun on her heel, keeping her eyes shut. Why on earth was he naked, it was so cold!

'Sorry, sir. No one answered the door.'

Sir? Since when did she call him sir? It was always a casual Brett in the office. But here that seemed too intimate. How many times had she dreamed of seeing the muscles that flexed beneath his suit laid bare? Of locking his office door and sprawling herself across his desk? Sir, indeed.

'Liana? What are you doing here?'

Was his voice always so deep?

'You can turn around now, I've got a towel on.'

He sounded amused—as if travelling all this way for a stupid signature was funny. She cracked open her eyes and turned slowly. She let out a low breath. Brett Buchanan in a towel wasn't a whole lot more decent than Brett Buchanan naked. If anything, that soft trail of down travelling from his navel to his—Eyes up! Stick to the plan. In and out. Oh Jeez.

Liana didn't know what had come over her. She'd seen

Brett Buchanan a hundred times at the office. His hazel eyes peered at her from underneath a lock of dishevelled honey coloured hair; hair that was never a strand out of place in the office. She pulled her jacket tighter around her chest, hoping he couldn't see her nipples harden through the thin blouse. She blamed the cold.

The bubbling sound had stopped. It was a spa bath behind him turned still, steaming. His skin glistened where the water still clung in drops.

Apologise for interrupting... Signature... Airport.

'Sorry, but this needed to be signed and witnessed today. You couldn't be reached.'

'That was the point,' he said. His gaze hardened for a moment, then softened. 'Come inside. You're half-frozen already. Do you even have stockings on?'

Thank heavens, she'd shaved her legs. She felt them shake beneath her, but was it cold or his gaze on them? He turned and walked towards the back door of the cottage. There were those broad shoulders again, bare and muscled.

Signature! She reminded herself. Signature, then leave.

She felt something soft land on her forehead. Then another on the back of her hand, and again on her nose.

Brett paused with his hand on the door handle and looked up smiling. 'The first snowfall.'

She followed his gaze and a flake landed on her lips. It melted and she stuck out her tongue to taste it. It thrilled her. She didn't feel as cold anymore. When she came to her senses she noticed he was staring at her face.

'I've never seen snow before,' she said, in defence mode. It was like she was stuck on autopilot. Defensive that the Board had sent her. Defensive that she had nothing better to do. Defensive that she was suddenly in the middle of nowhere with her crush of four years standing half-naked in front of her.

He startled. 'Really?'

'Never made it out here in winter before. Beach girl.' She would have face palmed if he wasn't still watching her. Beach girl? She looked back out over the valley of tree tops that fell sharply away from the edge of the property. The snow fell like icing sugar over the green and brown foliage. 'It's beautiful.'

'Let's get inside before it gets too heavy,' he said, huskily. He held the door open for her to walk past.

She took a deep breath and tried not to feel the heat radiating from his bare torso as she stepped inside the kitchen. It matched the rustic exterior stylistically, but with all the modern conveniences. Old timber bench tops around the room were complemented by a timber island in the centre of the room lined with breakfast stools. Brett strode over to put the kettle on, before turning to lean with his back to the bench, arms folded. He wasn't tanned—too many hours in the office—but the muscles across his chest and shoulders were well-defined. She wanted to run her nails across them. His cobalt gaze appraised her.

'You want me to sign something. What is so important it couldn't wait a week?'

She put down her bag and laid out the folder open to the first page.

'The contract for the purchase of the old Atari mine in Queensland. The higher bidder can't complete for twelve months, but we can complete in six. Atari have agreed to sell it to us, but only if we can sign the contract today and have the deposit to them by close of business tomorrow.'

He shook his head, grimacing. The honey forelock fell into his eyes and he pushed it back.

'John sent you all the way out here because I wasn't answering my phone?'

She hesitated. 'The Board agreed.'

'Right, and you drew the short straw?'

She pushed her hair back behind her ears. The comment hit home. Short straw or only straw more like it. They'd backed her into a corner.

'Don't you have someone waiting for you at home?'

She stuck out her chin, barriers up full shield, so he couldn't see the fantasy image burned behind her retinas of him standing wrapped in a towel in her own kitchen, after they had just...

'No, actually.' There. It was out now. Everyone at Buchanan officially knew she had no life: John, the Board, the CEO.

The kettle finished boiling. He prepared two red cups sitting on matching saucers on a wooden tray and produced two large cookies from a side jar.

'Hope you like chocolate chip. Milk? Sugar?'

Liana paused. Her senses were in disarray. He was making her tea, dressed only in a towel. 'Two sugars, please.'

He dutifully measured out two heaped teaspoons into the cup that was for her. 'Do you have a pen?'

'Of course.' She witnessed him sign the papers. Their hands brushed as he returned the pen for her to sign. She could smell the chlorine on his skin.

'You're freezing.' He placed his hand on her arm. The light caught gold flecks in his eyes. She leaned against the bench for support. 'There's a fire in the front room.'

He carried the tea tray through the side door. Closing the folder, she followed him. The documents were signed. There was no reason for her to stay any longer. He clearly wanted to be alone, hiding himself so far away. She had a flight to catch, documents to deliver. Get in, get out. Back on the road.

That was the plan.

But, he'd made her tea. She couldn't leave just yet. Her mind was spiralling back four years to that first day in the office, when they'd met. She'd gone home terrified that everyone knew that the blush on her face was not just first day jitters. He'd placed a hand on her arm then too—a welcome gesture that had set her skin alight.

The front room had the most comfortable-looking brown leather lounges draped in warm woollen blankets, all facing the large fireplace. The wooden mantel above it was dark from years of flames. Family photos lined it, small children playing in the garden of the cottage, among the roses—so unlike the formal portraits on his desk at work.

Brett stoked the embers of the fire and placed another log on top. 'Take a seat.' He rubbed the back of his neck. 'I should put some clothes on.'

Or take more off? She bit her lip and nodded, not trusting herself to speak. She moved closer to the fire and warmed herself. Outside, the snow was getting heavier. She looked at her watch. Fifteen minutes had passed since she'd left the car. How was that possible? How long had she stood outside staring up at the falling snow before remembering where she was and who was watching her?

———

BRETT SHUT the door to his bedroom and caught a glimpse of himself in the mirror. Not red, good. But, sweaty and... he pulled himself up short. It didn't matter. Liana was an employee. Office or cottage, it shouldn't be any different. He shouldn't want to grab her and kiss her the moment she turned those big doe eyes him. Caramel, he could never tell back in Sydney, under the harsh office lights, but watching the snowflake melt on her lips, the look of pure delight on her face at seeing her first snowfall... Definitely caramel.

Damn the Board. He'd come here to get away for a week. He was exhausted. The last thing he wanted to do was think about work. The company had consumed him night and day for the last year, ever since his mother had died. It was her company; she'd started it forty years prior. He was determined not to fail her, but he needed a break. He pulled on a casual pair of chinos and a t-shirt. He spritzed his hair back and dabbed a spot of cologne under his jaw, frowning into the mirror.

Liana.

Damn John. His CFO knew then. He had to. Why else would he send her specifically? Sneaky bastard. John had been his mother's closest adviser when she ran the company, and had always kept a close eye on Brett's career and private life.

Brett had tried to be discreet with his crush, he didn't have the time for it, and was firmly against dating staff. It contradicted company policy, his mother's policy, his policy. He had felt so transparent asking her if anyone was waiting at home. He crushed his hand into a fist. Now she was here, alone with him, and all he wanted to do was unwrap that thin coat of hers and... he shook the thought away and returned to the front room.

She was seated on the sofa closest to the fire, cradling the tea to her lips.

She stood up when she saw him. 'I'm much warmer now.' She put the half-drunk tea down on the table. 'I really need to be going or I'll miss my flight back. Thank you for signing the documents, for the tea and the fire...'

He was stunned. She was leaving already? She had

hold of her bag and was making for the door. He reached for her arm and she looked up at him, molten caramel. He couldn't keep her there. His thumb brushed along the inside of her elbow.

'Let me walk you to your car.'

He shoved his feet into his boots and pulled on his overcoat. His mother's coat still hung on the hook beside it. It still smelled of her favourite rose scent. He offered it to Liana and the spare boots too.

'It's only a few feet,' she said. He shook his head. It was the same fiery stubbornness she wielded in the office. He couldn't look at her again. If he looked at her again, he'd kiss her. He looked out the window instead and saw the snow burying deeper around them. It was cold enough that a thin layer coated the ground. Then he noticed her tyres.

'You haven't got the chains on.'

She blinked up at him.

'Excuse me?'

'Chains … you know, snow chains, for the tyres.'

Comprehension dawned on her face and her eyes flew open wider than before.

'The sign,' she said.

He cocked his head.

'The sign saying, "Chains required beyond this point". I saw it a short way back, but I thought it was a practical joke!' She laughed.

'You've never been to the snow before.' He grinned. She was so beautiful when she was confused. He adored both halves of her: the clever office dynamo who could burn him with a look, and the ingénue who melted him instead. In this moment, in this place, she was completely disarmed and so was he. 'You need chains on the tyres for extra grip. It stops them slipping on snow and black ice.'

'But, ice isn't black.'

That incredulous look again. Before he could stop himself, he'd bent down and pressed his lips against hers. She tasted of snow and sugared tea and she was wonderfully warm from the fire. When she leaned deeper into the kiss, he realised what he was doing and pulled away.

'I'm sorry.' He took a full step back from her and the howling wind that filled his body was colder than the snow outside. 'I shouldn't have done that. Let me see if I can find you some chains.' He turned sharply on his heel and left her standing there alone.

LIANA'S FINGERS flew to her lips in shock. He'd kissed her. Brett Buchanan had kissed her and she had kissed him back.

Did he always put on cologne when he was alone in his cottage? Her mind buzzed. She licked her lips and tasted the chlorine from the spa, which reminded her of his back and his butt and—when was the last time she'd been properly kissed? She'd been so busy with work, and so distracted crushing on him, she hadn't been playing the field lately.

The sound of clanging metal approached. Brett held loops of chains in gloved hands. They weren't chains in the sense she had imagined. She started at the thought and clasped her wrists tightly to stop herself thinking about Brett chaining her up with them and trailing kisses down her neck and below.

Boss! Signature… Flight… Atari mine.

Shit, the Atari mine, she'd completely forgotten. If she missed her flight, they'd lose the mine.

'Thank you for the chains,' she said, pointedly ignoring the tingle that still graced her lips and the warmth pooling in her belly. 'I'll make sure Atari get the documents.'

'I don't know if these will fit, but they're all I've got.' Brett averted his gaze.

He opened the door and a blast of cold air flew in, carrying with it a flurry of snowflakes. She changed her mind and donned the coat. The scent of roses brought back memories of her first day at Buchanan, meeting Liz, Brett's mother and the former CEO. She knew immediately whose coat it was and who had once tended the cottage garden. Liz had been her mentor both on a professional and personal level.

Was that why he was here? It had been a year and he never stopped. After the funeral, he'd thrown himself into his work. How many times had they stayed back late nutting out some deal or another. She braced herself and stepped out into the cold again.

Brett was kneeling in the snow laying out the chains in front of the two front wheels.

'I need you to move the car forward a few inches onto the chains.'

She nodded, teetering forward on her heels. Damn him, she wished she'd switched into the boots. She slid behind the wheel and dialled up the heating against her bare legs. He motioned her forward. She watched him squatted again before the front wheel. He tried to fit the chain to the tyre, but it wouldn't go. The chains seemed too small. He dusted the snow off his knees and picked the chains back up.

'You can't drive in this weather without chains. It's not safe. The Atari mine will have to wait.' He still wouldn't look her in the eye.

'What if we lose it?'

'Then we lose it. There will always be another deal. I'll

explain what happened to the Board. Let's get inside before we freeze.'

Following Brett back to the house, her heel slid sideways and she fell. He dropped the chains and rushed to her side. She shoved her bare hands into the snowy gravel and pushed herself up, ignoring his offer for help, but when she went to take a step, a sharp pain shot through her ankle and she faltered. He caught her by the elbow and helped her back inside to a seat on the stairs, slamming the door behind them.

Liana winced as she eased the heel off. She couldn't tell if the blue was from the cold or a bruise.

'I'll get ice.'

She laughed. 'I'm cold enough. I've just turned it. Give it a few minutes.'

The touch of his hand on her ankle sent shivers to her core. He gently turned it one way then another.

'Looks like a sprain to me. I'm getting that ice.'

He disappeared into the kitchen. She took off her other heel for balance and hopped into the front room, grabbing hold of the door frame and nearby furniture. She couldn't put any weight on the ankle. So graceful, she chastised herself. Maybe he was right. If it was sprained, she wouldn't be able to drive even if the weather did clear.

He put the ice on the coffee table, next to the abandoned tea and cookies, and offered her his arm to help her around the sofa.

'You don't have a car.'

'Derek dropped me off. I gave him the week holiday.'

'No phone, no internet?'

'Not that kind of holiday.'

Liana shrugged off the rose-scented coat and he took it off her to hang back up.

'She was an amazing woman,' Liana said. 'I miss having her around.'

He looked her in the eye then, for the first time since he'd kissed her.

'She built that company up from nothing,' he said.

'I know.' She settled into the sofa and combed her fingers through her loose hair, catching at the melting snow. 'I'm sorry for the drama: the chains, the ankle. The Board thought—I thought—I'd only be a few hours. I'm going to miss my flight.'

'It doesn't matter.'

'Atari...'

'None of it matters.'

There was something dark in his eyes that silenced her. She licked her lips, remembering the kiss again. The fire spiralled to life behind him. He propped her ankle on the coffee table and gently leaned the bag of ice against it.

'You didn't drink your tea.'

'I'll brew a fresh pot.' He picked up one of the woollen blankets and laid it over her before leaving her alone by the fire.

IN THE KITCHEN, Brett reset the kettle and let out a deep breath. He couldn't keep hiding from her. At some point he was going to have to sit down and talk to her about that kiss. That one heart-stopping kiss.

Only he didn't want to talk. Checking her ankle, he had wanted to slide his hand up the smooth length of her leg, past her knees and beneath her skirt. The hint of her thigh had driven him wild. She couldn't have noticed how her skirt had hiked up. She was in pain, and all he could think about was his hardening cock.

He checked the fridge and the pantry; they had enough food to last them the week if it came to it. He grabbed the ibuprofen.

He'd forgotten how close his mother had been to Liana. Liz had made a point of mentoring women in the firm and Liana had shown great potential. If his mother had still been alive and CEO, Liana would have been promoted by now. But he'd let things like that slide. He was too busy trying to keep it all together, he'd forgotten the first lesson his mother ever taught him: to value his people.

'I found painkillers in the pantry.' He put down the tray and sat down beside her. He dipped a cookie into his tea and it half crumbled into the cup.

'Thanks!'

'I'm afraid I've let a few things slip at Buchanan.'

She sat up taller, frowning at him. The blanket fell from her chest and he had to force himself to look up.

'What? No.'

'The employee mentoring and support groups. I need to pay more attention to the people.' Especially their faces, he thought, her blouse left little to the imagination.

'It's fine. Everyone has stepped up.' She placed a hand over his in the space between them on the sofa. 'You didn't even take time to grieve.'

'There was work to do.' He felt the raspy burn-out in his voice. He shut his eyes and laid back on the sofa. Her hand was still covering his, small and warm.

'And now there's not.'

He heard the smile in her voice. Maybe he could convince her to stay the week. He breathed deeply, allowing the corners of his own mouth to lift up too.

'There's not a drop of work to be done, and no way to do it if there was,' she mused. 'I can see why you chose here as your escape.'

He froze, eyes flying open, as she pressed a finger against his lips. She hovered above him, staring into his eyes, searching for something. Then she smiled, shut her eyes, and replaced her finger with her lips. He was lost in her eyelashes and the soft touch of her lips moving against his. Her tongue flicked against him and he opened his mouth to let her in.

———

LIANA WAS SINKING DEEPER into the sofa, pulling him to her. The fire, the tea, the scent of his cologne, and underneath it all, the familiar raw scent of him that made her dizzy in the office; all her usual defences had crumbled away like the cookie in the tea. When they paused for breath, she pulled away, and pressed her fingers to her lips.

'I shouldn't have done that.' She echoed his words from earlier.

'I've wanted to do that for four years.'

She stared at him uncomprehending for a few moments. His gaze was steady, honest. This was her boss, her Brett.

'Four?'

He nodded. She scrambled for a brick in her defences, but they'd all fallen down and wouldn't move back into place.

'Then why didn't you?' she challenged, lips still slightly parted and throbbing.

'Because there are rules in the office. Rules I agreed to abide by. Rules that you agreed to as well.'

'Rules that…' She licked her lips. 'Don't apply here?'

He hung his head and groaned. His honey hair brushed against her cheek.

'I really hope not.'

She laughed and kissed the top of his head. Four years. He'd wanted her just as she had wanted him. They'd wasted four years of kisses hotter than the fire that blazed behind them.

'I hope not, too.'

He looked up at her.

'You're injured and stranded, and I don't want you to think I'm taking advantage.'

'After four years? After those kisses? Brett.' She bristled at the suggestion. 'If I was able to walk, I'd be putting those snow chains to a different use right now.'

She was rewarded with a deep warm laugh. The kind she hadn't heard him issue in years. He ran his hands through her hair pulling her face closer. She gripped his biceps tightly and kissed him again. He pulled away and cupped her chin in his hand, gazing into her eyes hungrily.

'If we kiss again,' he said. 'I'm not going to be able to stop.'

Her breath came in heavy. 'Don't then, four years is long enough.'

She pressed her forehead to the curve of his neck and kissed the line of his collarbone.

He picked her up and laid her lengthways on the sofa, carefully arranging her ankle on a cushion. She started to undo her blouse, but he stopped her and took over, kissing the skin revealed beneath each button to her navel.

He shucked his t-shirt next and with his hand on his belt buckle he hesitated.

'Condom?'

'I haven't carried one in a while.'

'Let me go check,' He ran a hand through his unruly hair and jogged to the bedroom. A few moments later he came out with a box. 'Close to expiry but still good.'

Liana had shucked her skirt and lay there in her bra

and knickers. He took a moment to stare at her apprecia-tively, before bending to her waist to tug down the lace. He kissed her inner thighs, the space below her belly button, her hips. He traced his lips and his fingers everywhere, except for her centre.

She dug one hand in his shoulder and buried the other in his hair. He finally removed her undies completely and bent his lips to the wetness beneath.

She writhed as he flicked his tongue and thrust his fingers, massaging her gently, bringing her to the brink and then drawing away to play again at kissing and touching her around her clit and not on it. She moaned for him and he bent his head to bring her to the edge again, but no further. Her whole body was tensed.

He stood up and shook his pants to the floor. She admired him in full and reached for him as he slid the condom on. He straddled her on the sofa and lowered his weight to kiss her gently about her neck and her breasts. There was tenderness in his every movement. Her heart had never beat so fast, it was full to bursting. Brett wanted her every bit as much as she had wanted him. Four years, she marvelled.

He pulled her bra aside and sucked on her nipples, sending one hand back down her belly to stroke her. She pulled on his cock, demanding more. He raised his head to kiss her deeply on the mouth and, mid-kiss, he entered her. He was slow at first, but she wrapped her hands around his buttocks to draw him further in. They began to rock, faster and faster, the tension building between them till it spilled over and they cried out in unison, grabbing each other, holding on through the spasms, her ankle forgotten. There was only the bliss of the moment.

After, they lay still, breathing heavily, embracing each other.

'I think your tea's gone cold,' Liana said.

'I'm not interested in tea.' He nipped at her neck, growling softly. 'What were you saying about those chains?'

She laughed and the movement pressed their bodies together again. She could feel them both reawakening. The want expanded, finally free after four years shackled behind office protocols. Her heart expanded right along with it.

'Well, boss, why don't you get them and we find out?'

Little Gems

_____

Want to try something a little sweeter?
Why not try our Little Gems Anthology?

LITTLE GEMS 2018:
JADE

Little Gems anthologies can be purchased from the
Romance Writers of Australia store
http://romanceaustralia.com/shop/

Spicy Bites 2019

The theme for the 2019 Spicy Bites anthology will be…

MASKS

For details of how to submit a story, please see Romance Writers of Australia's website http://romanceaustralia.com/contests/aspiring-contests/spicy-bites/

Previous Spicy Bites anthologies can be purchased from the Romance Writers of Australia store http://romanceaustralia.com/shop/

About the Authors

Josie Baker

Josie Baker is a connoisseur of beauty and sensuality. She collects scintillating vignettes on her travels as inspiration for her stories, her imagination weaving in an extra dose of romance and passion. Josie's writing offers sensuous glimpses into the lives of 'ordinary' women.

'Love, Lust & Nipples Clamps', is a collection of Josie's short stories and novelettes, reminiscent of Anais Nin's 'Little Birds'. Each story will take you on an erotic journey. Available at Amazon.

Join Josie as she shares her sensual discoveries on her blog www.josiebaker.exposed

Sonia Caine

Sonia Caine is a contemporary romance writer also writing under the name Sonia Stanizzo. She lives in the beautiful South Coast of New South Wales with her childhood sweetheart/husband and their three children. When she's not dreaming up stories about couples and their road to finding love – sometimes bumpy but always a lot of fun –

she can be found taking pole dancing lessons (purely for the fun and exercise), reading and writing.

C M James

C M James thought she was a YA science fiction and fantasy writer who liked to blow things up or fly in the dragon cavalry. But then her characters grew older and liked to get a little bit naughty between the sheets, and out of them. Now C follows the characters and the idea and worries about where the story 'fits' later. The dragons still fly fiercely by her side. She lives in Sydney's East with her inspirational hubby, Mr James, and dreams of a house down south with dogs and babies.

Suzie Jay

Adelaide author Suzie Jay grew up within walking distance from the beach, dreaming of life as a famous author or Johnny Farnham's back-up singer. After a stint as a teacher and stay at home mum, she decided to make her dream a reality, writing romance – not singing, because she can't hold a tune. She didn't give up on Johnny all together and in her spare time sings along to 80's hits, bakes and binges on Netflix with her knight in shining armour- who's more likely to wear tattered footy jumpers than chainmail.

Visit www.suziejayauthor.com Twitter: @suziejayauthor
Facebook: https://www.facebook.com/suziejayauthor/
Instagram: https://www.instagram.com/suziejayauthor/

Emma Lea

Emma Lea loves a good happy ending.

Emma loves to read and write romance. She is the author of The Young Royals, a sweet romance series set in a small, fictitious European country, and The Young Billionaires, a hot and sexy contemporary romance series set in Australia.

Emma has lived a nearly thirty-year love story with her husband whom she adores. They are recent empty-nesters and live on the beautiful Sunshine Coast in Queensland, Australia along with a cat named Coco and a dog named Star. She has two adult sons who have embarked on their own lifelong romances.

Fiona Marsden

Fiona M Marsden started out as an avid reader. She was a late starter in finding romance novels, but once found, they became an addiction. Considering she wrote poetry and stories from a young age, it was only logical that the next step would be to write her own romances.

Published Work:
"Medal Up" 2018
"The Runaway Christmas Elf," 2017
"Swept Away & Road Trip Baby" Li Family Duology, 2017
"The Jaded Rake", Little Gems Anthology 2018, RWAus

"Heart of Stone", Little Gems Anthology 2017, RWAus.
"The Sunstone Bride", "The Sunstone Inheritance", Little
Gems Short Story Anthology 2016, RWAus.
www.fionamarsden.com

Melanie Page

Melanie Page found her HEA in the Eighties. Since then,
she's raised an awesome brood, got a couple of degrees
and taken up lion taming (sorry, high school teaching…
same thing). As a budding writer, she finished her first
novel 'An Affair of Honour', created a Kindle account and
pressed publish. She's since learned better.

Although her first love is Regency, Melanie has since
moved into Fantasy and Steampunk, co-authoring 'Iron
Heart' with MC D'Alton. When not teaching, or arranging
HEAs for all her fictional friends, she likes to travel with
her husband or play with her grandchildren.

C.L. Rose

Books and reading have always been a big part of C.L.
Rose's life. She has been collecting ideas for stories her
entire life, now she finally has time to write them. She is
married, loves camp fires, cooking and red wine, not neces-
sarily in that order. This is her first published story, and she
has many more to come.

Shannon Slique

Shannon Slique lives on the southern end of the Gold Coast in Queensland where she could spend her days drinking tea and watching the tides come and go – if only reality didn't intrude. She travels a lot with her husband and that gives her insight into interesting locations for her stories – both in Australia and overseas. Shannon loves writing erotica, first because it deepens a romantic relationship between her characters and, then, just for the cheeky naughtiness of it.

Wren St Claire

Wren St Claire lives in Brisbane with her husband, two elderly miniature Schnauzers and two mad Bengal cats. She has more Master's degrees than is healthy for one person to have, including an MA in Egyptology. She loves reading and writing and gets grumpy and sad when she can't write. She has too many story ideas and characters running round her head. Alpha in Chains is her first foray in to Sci Fi Romance, look for a series inspired by this story.

Visit her website and sign up for freebies on her giveaway list www.wrenstclaire.com. She won't spam you, promise. She is a founding member of the Bookbaybz, a group of Brisbane based romance writers and the most awesome women she knows. www.bookbaybz.com

Davina Stone

Davina Stone wrote and illustrated her first novel at the ripe age of twelve. She spent her early years reading romances and practising kissing techniques on the back of her hand while waiting for her prince to arrive.

Eventually he did, whisking her from England to Australia on his motorbike. After a varied career she now devotes herself to honing her romance writing skills. Davina resides on the beautiful West Australian coast surrounded by a large crazy family and her muse, a small black dog who helps her to concoct plots on their daily walks together. Website: www.davinastone.com

S.E. Welsh

S.E. Welsh is a self-confessed bibliophile who moonlights as a writer, when her day jobs of Secondary Teacher and Mother allow. A two-time winner of the Northern Territory Literary Awards and finalist in the IEUA Queensland and Northern Territory Literary Competition, her short and flash fiction, under an alternate pen name, have been highly acclaimed.

Welsh's poetry has been electronically published by The Red Room Company and her short fiction features in a variety of anthologies. More recently, she has been exploring both the romance and speculative fiction genres. Worlds within worlds and happily ever after's are proving both exciting and challenging for the fun-loving wordsmith.